FORT WORTH LIBRARY

KEITH

3 1668 05910 2126

• • • • • •

She stepped out of the dressing room grinning from ear to ear. Aunt Mary's face lit up as well.

"Oh, wow, Serena! That dress is *gorgeous*!"

"I know," Serena said, and she did a little twirl. "I love it!"

Her aunt stepped closer to scrutinize the outfit more closely. She slipped a finger under the waistband and said, "This size might be *too* perfect. I don't know how comfortable you'll be, after you eat dinner that night. Your belly's getting a little pudgy."

Serena blushed, and her smile retreated for a moment. She felt like her aunt could feel the tiny, new life growing beneath the dress' waistband.

"I'm just a little bloated," she said. "You know how it is..."

"Oh, well I'm sure it'll be fine, then," Mary said.

Serena's smile was back, but her face burned, and she felt perspiration accumulating on her forehead. She knew her aunt thought she was referring to her menstrual cycle. That lie would definitely come back to haunt her. When Serena finally told the truth, Aunt Mary would wonder how she got so far along in her pregnancy, if she was still menstruating when they shopped for her prom dress.

But the lie was out now, and there was no way to take it back. Serena sucked her stomach in a little until her aunt completed her inspection.

"Looks like this is the one," Mary told the clerk. "How much is it?"

Serena was surprised to hear the question. She thought her aunt would've made sure they could afford it before she let her try it on.

"Three-fifty," the clerk said right away.

Serena's heart squeezed uncomfortably. She looked down at her feet in embarrassment.

But Aunt Mary said, "We'll take it," and her heart was light again.

• • • • • •

W0011005

PROM NIGHT AT FINLEY HIGH

PROM NIGHT

AT FINLEY HIGH

KEITH THOMAS WALKER

KEITHWALKERBOOKS, INC
This is a UMS production

PROM NIGHT AT FINLEY HIGH

KEITHWALKERBOOKS

Publishing Company
KeithWalkerBooks, Inc.
P.O. Box 331585
Fort Worth, TX 76163

All rights reserved. Except for use in any review, the reproduction or utilization of this manuscript in whole or partial in any form by any mechanical, electronic, or other means, not known or hereafter invented, including photocopying, xerography, and recording, or in any information retrieval or storage system, is forbidden without written permission of the publisher, KeithWalkerBooks, Inc.

For information write
KeithWalkerBooks, Inc.
P.O. Box 331585
Fort Worth, TX 76163

All characters in this book have no existence outside the imagination of the author and have no relation whatsoever to anyone bearing the same name or names. They are not even distantly inspired by any individual known or unknown to the author and all incidents are pure invention.

Copyright © 2015 Keith Thomas Walker

ISBN-13 DIGIT: 978-0-9882180-7-9
ISBN-10 DIGIT: 0988218070
Library of Congress Control Number: 2015901683
Manufactured in the United States of America

First Edition

Visit us at www.keithwalkerbooks.com

KEITH THOMAS WALKER

This book is for the Twinkie Twins
Rachel and Anna

Congratulations to Jasmine Walker whose first published poems
Mirror Mirror and *No One Can Ever Know* are proudly featured
in this novel. You go girl!

MORE BOOKS BY
KEITH THOMAS WALKER

Fixin' Tyrone
How to Kill Your Husband
A Good Dude
Riding the Corporate Ladder
The Finley Sisters' Oath of Romance
Blow by Blow
Jewell and the Dapper Dan
Harlot
Plan C (And More KWB Shorts)
Dripping Chocolate
The Realest Ever
Jackson Memorial
Sleeping With the Strangler
Life After
Blood for Isaiah
Brick House
Brick House 2

NOVELLAS

Might be Bi (Part One)
Harder

POETRY COLLECTION

Poor Righteous Poet

FINLEY HIGH SERIES

Prom Night at Finley High

Visit keithwalkerbooks.com for information about
these and upcoming titles from KeithWalkerBooks

ACKNOWLEGMENTS

Of course I would like to thank God, first and foremost, for giving me the creativity and drive to pursue my dreams and the understanding that I am nothing without Him. I would like to thank my wife for being my first and most important critic, and I would like to thank my mother for always pushing me to be the best I can be. I would like to thank Janae Hampton for being the best advisor, supporter and little sister a brother could ever have. I would also like to thank (in no particular order) Denise Bolds, Sabrina Scott, Beulah Neveu, Jason Owens, Sharon Blount, BRAB Book Club, and Uncle Steven Thomas, one love. I'd like to thank everyone who purchased and enjoyed one of my books. Everything I do has always been to please you. I know there are folks who mean the world to me that I'm failing to mention. I apologize ahead of time. Rest assured I'm grateful for everything you've done for me!

PROM NIGHT AT FINLEY HIGH

CHAPTER ONE
DADDY'S LITTLE GIRL

Serena stared down at the three, crisp one hundred dollar bills and the handwritten letter her aunt gave her. Aunt Mary looked over at her and smiled briefly, before returning her attention to the freeway. Aunt Mary drove a Jeep Patriot. It wasn't new, but she kept it clean, and it was one of the best vehicles Serena had the pleasure of riding in on a regular basis.

She looked up from the goodies her Aunt gave her, her eyes knitted in confusion. Her heart rate steadily picked up speed. Aunt Mary had told her about the money already, but Serena didn't really believe it. In all eighteen years of her short life, she'd never touched a one hundred dollar bill that fully belonged to her. Now she had three of them. She was suddenly anxious, as if she had done something illegal to obtain the funds.

"How?" she asked. "Where did he get this from?"

Serena and her aunt were travelling five miles under the speed limit on Interstate 20, because it was Saturday afternoon, and seemingly everyone in the great city of

Overbrook Meadows had somewhere to be today. The date was May 2nd. The springtime weather was beautiful. Serena planned to take her brother and sisters to the park when she got home. Hopefully she would have enough money left to buy them a few cheap kites from the dollar store. It was a little windy, and kite-flying was a regular activity that would make Serena feel like her family was regular, for a little while at least.

In response to her question, her aunt shrugged and then shook her head. Mary was a thin woman with soft features that were generally cheerful and always empathetic. Serena didn't think she had ever seen her angry, but the look she wore now was all too familiar. Aunt Mary looked disappointed, yet grateful at the same time. Serena knew that the money was the cause of her inner turmoil.

"I don't know where he got it from," she replied. "I could guess, but I don't suppose any of that matters now. The important thing is he wanted you to have that money, and he made a way to get it to you. Put me in a very uncomfortable situation, but it's done now."

Serena knew her aunt was trying to drop the conversation, but she was very curious about all things related to her father.

"But how did he get it to you?"

Aunt Mary frowned and didn't immediately respond, as if divulging this information might corrupt Serena in some way.

"I bought him a bag of chips," she revealed. "I watched him eat them. When our visit was almost over, he gave the bag back to me and told me to take it home and give it to you. Of course I was confused by that, but he stopped me before I could look in the bag. He said, '*Don't open it in here. Just ball it up and leave with it, like you're going to throw it away.'*

"I was scared," Aunt Mary confided, "because I could feel something in the bag then, and I knew it wasn't no chips. I looked around, and it felt like every guard in there was watching us. I told him, *'Pat, what kind of mess you trying to get me caught up in?'* He said, *'This is for Serena's prom. Please, Mary. I won't never ask you to do nothing like this again.'*

"So I took the bag," Mary said, *"for you.* And that's what I found in it when I got in the car; that money and that letter. I'm still mad at Pat for doing that to me without any warning, but I guess it is for a good cause. Nothing he did with the money in jail would've been any good..."

Mary's explanation raised as many questions as it answered. Serena's father was in prison – had been since she was two years old. Serena hated to admit it, but she didn't have any memories of her dad that didn't involve him being locked up. Patrick, or *Big Pat,* as he was affectionately known, was currently serving twenty years for armed robbery and drug possession with the intent to deliver.

Almost everyone in Serena's family seemed to take pride in Patrick's past when they talked about him. According to her mother, Big Pat was a hustler and a playboy. When he was on the streets, he ran several successful dope houses.

Aunt Mary saw her brother-in-law in a different light. She said Patrick got his twenty-year sentence because he was reckless and irresponsible, and he never took his education seriously.

According to Patrick himself, he was a victim of society. He told Serena that America's war on drugs was really just a war on poor black and brown people. He said a judicial system set up to give drug dealers more time in prison than murderers got was obviously flawed.

Serena's opinion of her father was somewhere in the middle of all of that. She did think the laws that kept minorities imprisoned for twenty years or more for drug offenses were unjust. But her father wasn't only convicted for drug pedaling. He robbed people too.

Serena had a gun pointed at her face once, and she still considered it one of the most horrifying experiences of her life. In her opinion, the person who did that to her deserved to be in prison for a long time. And if her father did that to someone else, then maybe his time in prison was also justified.

But regardless of what got him there, Serena knew that her father continued to hustle while incarcerated. Inmates were not allowed to have cellphones in any Texas penitentiary, but Big Pat had one. He used it to call his daughter sometimes.

She loved to hear from him, but the calls also spooked her a little. The reception was never stellar, so Serena spent most of their conversations saying, "Daddy, I can't hear you." It was always a risk when Pat had to raise his voice, because there might be guards around who would hear him and confiscate his phone. He was supposed to get out in a couple of years. Serena knew that her father could get more time added to his sentence if he got caught with a cellphone.

And if Big Pat was able to come up with three hundred dollars cash in an environment where no inmate was allowed to have actual currency, then he was probably selling drugs again. Of course that could get him more time in prison as well.

Serena understood why her aunt was apprehensive about the money, because she felt the same way. But Serena was much younger and less mature than Aunt Mary. She quickly decided that the goal completely outweighed the risks her father took when he smuggled the cash out of prison. She desperately needed the money, and she had no way of getting it without him. Overall Big Pat was probably a bad parent, but this afternoon he was in the running for a Father of the Year award.

"This is all mines?" she asked her aunt, a slight smile creeping to her face.

Aunt Mary looked over at her, and she smiled as well. "Yes, baby. It's all yours. Your father was very adamant about me giving it to you and *only* you."

"You saw him this morning?"

Aunt Mary nodded. "Yes. I've been on the road all day." She yawned. "I'm pretty tired now, to tell you the truth."

Serena's smile slipped and was replaced with guilt. She hated to be a burden. "I'm sorry. I could've rode the bus."

"No, it's alright," Mary said. "It would be too hard to get your dress home on the bus."

Serena's smile returned at the mention of her dress.

"I won't need this much money, will I?"

Her aunt nodded. "Probably. Prom dresses are expensive. I don't think you'll find a nice one for less than two hundred dollars."

Serena's eyes widened. A field of goose bumps sprouted on her arms. As far as she could remember, she'd never spent more than $30 on any one item of clothing. The thought of dropping $200 on a dress that she would probably only wear once was ludicrous. But it was also amazing. It was like a fairy tale. This type of good fortune didn't happen to people like her – or at least it never had before.

"Mama didn't wanna go with you?" she asked.

Mary shook her head. "I didn't ask her. Like I said, Patrick wanted to make sure the money got to you. If he gave it to your mama, we both know that wouldn't have happened."

Serena did know that. And she knew her aunt really loved her, if she was willing to make a three hour drive to prison on a Saturday morning to visit a man who wasn't directly related to her.

"Thank you," she told her. "You don't know how much this means to me."

"Sure I do," Mary said. "I was once a senior in high school myself. I know how important this is."

Serena continued to smile, though she doubted if her aunt had ever felt what she was feeling right now. No one could understand how big prom night was to her. It would easily be the most extravagant date she had ever been on. But it was more than that. Serena knew that after she graduated high school in four weeks, her enjoyment of life would decline drastically. Considering that her life hadn't been so great up to now, the thought of it getting even worse was actually frightening.

But before the dark clouds converged over her and made themselves at home, Serena had one last chance to be carefree and enjoy the same things all of the normal kids took for granted. A week from today she would put on a beautiful dress and get a taste of what it was like to be a princess. The whole idea of prom night had begun to take on the quality of a fairy tale. Even with the money in her hand, Serena feared that fate might swoop in and dash all of her plans at the last minute.

She unfolded the letter Aunt Mary delivered with the money and recognized her father's neat handwriting. After nearly two decades behind bars, Big Pat's penmanship was impeccable. Even when he wrote on blank paper, like the letter Serena had now, his words flowed neatly on imaginary lines and did not exceed the paper's imaginary margins. His spelling wasn't the best, but if Serena could write half as neatly as her dad, it would cut down on a lot of the criticism she received from her English teacher at Finley High.

Her father wrote:

Hey, baby girl!

If you're reading this, then you got the money I sent with your aunt, and hopefully you're on your way to the store to buy that prom dress. I can't tell you how proud I am of you! My little girl isn't so little anymore. You're about to graduate high school and take the world by storm! I have so much faith in you. I know you can be whatever you decide you want to be in this world. You got the smarts and you got the potentual, and I know you have the drive and dedication.

I want you to pick out the best prom dress they have. If this isn't enough money, tell your aunt to give you whatever else you need, and I promise I'll give it back to her the next time I see her. I know you're going to be the prettiest girl there. Thank you for the picture you sent with your last letter. I stared at it all the time. It's hard to believe you grew up so quick. I hate that I missed so much of your life. I hope you know how beautiful you are.

I promise when I get out of here (which should be next year) I'm never coming back to this place. I'm going to do whatever I can to stay in your life even if it means I have to be a trashman. I'd rather have a regular job then to be in prison. I know you think I missed too much of your life already but I haven't. You still have a lot of things you need a daddy for, like when you need help with your first car or apartment. And when you get married, I _WILL_ be there to walk you down the aisle.

I hope the boy you're going to the prom with treats you with respect. I know you think you're grown, but you're still my little girl. Don't let anyone take advantage of you, just because they think your father is not around to protect you. When you send me pictures from your prom, make sure you send a picture of your date too.

One last thing. Thank you so much for proving people wrong. Since you grew up in the jets without a father in the house, you were supposed to have a baby before you graduated. It's not me saying that. It's statistic. But you proved those statistic wrong! It make me want to cry, when I think about how proud I am!

Have fun at the prom, baby girl! Don't never forget daddy loves you!

Patrick Massey

Serena felt sick to her stomach by the time she finished the letter, but that didn't stop her from reading it again. The letter hurt just as much the second time around – but not all of it. It was the last paragraph that tugged at her heart and made her feel like she'd let everyone down.

Since you grew up in the jets without a father in the house, you were supposed to have a baby before you graduated. But you proved those statistic wrong!

Her father was only half right about that, but he didn't have to know. Not right now, anyway. Serena would wait until after the prom before she broke his heart, just as she planned to tell everyone else – *after the prom*. She didn't think that was a selfish decision. Even if it was, she felt like she should be able to call the shots this one time. It was her life and her body after all.

Aunt Mary noticed Serena's change in demeanor as she read the letter, but she didn't ask what was wrong. Serena's father had been locked up since she was a toddler. The most Patrick could do to support his daughter as she grew into womanhood was write letters and smuggle ill-gotten money out of prison for her prom dress.

All things considered, Serena was one of the strongest people Mary knew. If the correspondence from her father broke her down a little bit, that was totally understandable. Mary knew that she would have suffered similar breakdowns far more often, if she was in her niece's shoes.

CHAPTER TWO
WINE BERRY PURPLE

Mirror, mirror on the wall
Look at me
I just wanna fall
See myself looking back at me
Wishing I could say one, two, three
And "POOF!"
You have a perfect face!
Yeah right. I wish. I'm such a disgrace
This is what I thought
When I was blue
But now I know the only beautiful thing is you
Yes, you, staring back at me
That pretty, vibrant girl
Can't you see?
You mean the world to someone
And when you feel blue
Look into this mirror and stare at that pretty girl
You

By Jasmine Walker

When they got to the mall, Aunt Mary surprised Serena by heading straight to Dillard's. That was one of the department stores that was generally off limits for Serena's family. Her mother didn't have a car, so their trips to the mall were already few and far between. On the rare occasions they did go, she would steer Serena and her siblings to more cost-efficient stores like Sears and Payless.

The last time Serena went to Dillard's, it was when a few of her girlfriends from the neighborhood hopped on a city bus one Saturday afternoon with no true goals in mind. Their mall loitering eventually led them to Dillard's, where the store clerks seemed to zero in on them within seconds. Toya, the unofficial leader of their crew, ended up cursing out the fifth associate who approached and asked, "May I help you with something?" All eyes were certainly on them at that point, and the girls left the store without parting with their measly dollars.

The same clerks were there when Serena and her aunt entered the store, but they were a lot more friendly and less confrontational today. Serena guessed it was because her aunt was an adult, and Mary didn't give off any low-class/thievery vibes. Plus Mary was a devout Christian who oozed honesty from her pores.

As they perused fancy aisles stocked with overpriced wares, Serena wished (not for the first time) that Mary was her mother, rather than Princess. She never lived with Mary, but she didn't have to live with her to know that her life would've gone down a much better path, compared to the predicament she was currently facing.

The folks at Dillard's had all of their prom dresses in one area in the women's department. When they got there, Serena felt like a chipmunk in a peanut factory. The mannequins were all petite, adorned with elegant gowns that came in every color of the rainbow. Some of the dresses were skin tight. Others were loose and flowing, with long slits that marched halfway up the thigh. Serena admired dresses that came with or without straps and sleeves. She fell in love with a red one that had a sweetheart neckline. It shimmered with sequins and beads that looked like pearls.

But she quickly forgot about that one when she saw the dress of her dreams. It was dark gray with a knee-length skirt that had ruffles and several overlapping layers. The bodice was low-cut and strapless, with intricate floral designs sewn in. Even better, the waistband was a beautiful, gleaming purple, which was Serena's favorite color.

As she admired it with wide eyes and parted lips, she knew that her date would love the dress as well. Jamar was the most conservative boy she knew. She didn't want to offend him with a low-cut neckline that would thrust her ample boobs in his face. She also didn't want to make him uncomfortable with one of the skin-tight gowns that looked like they could double for prostitute attire.

She turned to her aunt, her smile big and hopeful.

"This is the one I want!"

Aunt Mary also smiled as she admired the dress. "It's beautiful, Serena. But are you sure that's the one?"

"Yes! I'm sure. What's wrong? You don't like it?"

"Yes. I think it's gorgeous. But we've only been here a few minutes. Don't you want to look around a little more?"

Serena shook her head. "No. Purple's my favorite color. This dress is *perfect*."

"Okay," Aunt Mary said. "I think you made a great choice." She approached the mannequin and fingered the soft fabric on the skirt. She looked back at her niece and smiled. "I hope they have it in your size."

Serena's heart sank. She didn't realize that availability might be an issue. "Oh no. They gotta have it," she said with a frown.

"What size do you wear now?" her aunt asked, looking her up and down.

She almost said *eight*, but she knew that she'd gained a few pounds in the past couple of months. Some of the jeans she wore to school were fitting a little tight lately. Serena had no idea what size she was up to. She said, "Ten," thinking that was a safe guess.

"Okay, hold on a sec'," her aunt said and left in search of a salesperson.

Serena remained in her place and continued to admire the dress while she waited. She imagined herself wearing the dress and entering the prom arm in arm with her date. She had no idea what an actual prom looked like, but Serena pictured a huge ballroom with strobe lights and colorful streamers and balloons hanging from the ceiling. All of the students would be dressed like adults attending a wedding, and they would all stop and stare at Serena and her date. She and Jamar would stroll down a red carpet while underclassmen threw rose petals at their feet.

Rose petals?

Serena giggled at her own imagination. But reining in her expectations didn't take away from her excitement one iota. She was nearly bouncing with anxiety by the time her aunt returned with an associate who toted a hanger with a duplicate of the dress worn by the mannequin.

"You made an excellent choice," the clerk said with a pasted-on smile. "We only have two of these left in stock –

and only *one* size ten." She handed the dress to Serena. "You can try it on," she said. "The fitting rooms are right over here..."

Serena and her aunt followed the woman to the dressing rooms. She locked herself inside one of the stalls and said a quick prayer before she tried on the dress. She knew that God heard her because the dress fit her perfectly. She stared at her reflection in the large mirror and thought she looked amazing. Her honey brown skin glowed under the florescent lights, and the gown accented her womanly curves. She didn't even feel like herself in the dress. She knew she'd look even better once she styled her hair and put on a little makeup.

She stepped out of the dressing room grinning from ear to ear. Aunt Mary's face lit up as well.

"Oh, wow, Serena! That dress is *gorgeous!*"

"I know," Serena said, and she did a little twirl. "I love it!"

Her aunt stepped closer to scrutinize the outfit more closely. She slipped a finger under the waistband and said, "This size might be *too* perfect. I don't know how comfortable you'll be, after you eat dinner that night. Your belly's getting a little pudgy."

Serena blushed, and her smile retreated for a moment. She felt like her aunt could feel the tiny, new life growing beneath the dress' waistband.

"I'm just a little bloated," she said. "You know how it is..."

"Oh, well I'm sure it'll be fine, then," Mary said.

Serena's smile was back, but her face burned, and she felt perspiration accumulating on her forehead. She knew her aunt thought she was referring to her menstrual cycle.

That lie would definitely come back to haunt her. When Serena finally told the truth, Aunt Mary would wonder how she got so far along in her pregnancy, if she was still menstruating when they shopped for her prom dress.

But the lie was out now, and there was no way to take it back. Serena sucked her stomach in a little until her aunt completed her inspection.

"Looks like this is the one," Mary told the clerk. "How much is it?"

Serena was surprised to hear the question. She thought her aunt would've made sure they could afford it before she let her try it on.

"Three-fifty," the clerk said right away.

Serena's heart squeezed uncomfortably. She looked down at her feet in embarrassment.

But Aunt Mary said, "We'll take it," and her heart was light again.

"But I only have three hundred," she mumbled to her aunt.

"It's alright," Mary said. She reached and rubbed her shoulder affectionately. "I can take care of the rest."

"Great. I'll be right over here when you're ready," the saleswoman said before returning to her register.

● ● ● ● ● ●

When they got back to her aunt's car, Serena asked if she could use her phone to take a picture of the dress and send it to her date. She had a cellphone of her own, but it was a cheap, pre-paid model that didn't have a camera. For twenty dollars, she got sixty minutes of talk time, but her mother was adamant about those sixty minutes lasting a whole month.

"Just use it for *emergencies*," Princess had instructed her. "If you got something quick to tell somebody, you can use it for that. But don't be up on the phone all night, like it ain't nothing. If you wanna talk that long, use the house phone."

After she sent the picture to Jamar, Serena asked her aunt, "Do you mind if I call him?"

"No, of course not," Mary said as she backed out of her parking spot.

Serena dialed the number, and Jamar answered right away.

"Hello?"

"Hi. It's me, Serena."

"Oh, *Serena*. Hey, thanks for calling. I was wondering why some random person was sending me a picture of a dress."

She grinned. "Whatever. You knew it was me. So you got the pic'?"

"Yes. It looks pretty. I really like it."

"Me, too," Serena said. She couldn't stop smiling.

"What color is it?" he asked. "Black?"

"It's dark gray with a purple waistband."

"Should I get my cummerbund to match the waistband?"

"Yes, that's what the lady at the store said. She said to make sure to tell you it's *wine berry* purple."

"*Wine berry*? I never heard of that color before."

"Me neither," Serena said. "But I like it. Purple is my favorite color."

"I'll bet that dress looks great on you."

"It does. I tried it on."

"That's awesome. I'll tell my mom. I think she wants to go get my tux today."

"Alright."

"I'm excited. I can't wait 'til next Saturday."

"Me too. I'm in the car with my aunt right now. I'll call you later, when I get home."

"Okay. Talk to you later."

CHAPTER THREE
BIBLE BOY

When she returned the cellphone to her aunt, Serena noticed she had a peculiar expression.

"What?" she asked her.

"Nothing," Mary said. "Was that your date?"

"Yes," Serena said, still smiling. "That was Jamar."

"He's a senior, right?"

"Yeah. We both graduate this year."

Aunt Mary waited for her to divulge more, but Serena was waiting for another question.

After a few moments of silence, Serena said, "I guess you want to know more about him..."

"Oh, that would be nice," Mary said. She looked over at her niece with a smirk.

"I'm sure you'll love him," Serena said. "Next to you, I don't know anyone who goes to church more than Jamar."

Mary was confused by the comment, but she kept her mouth closed and let her niece tell the story.

• • • • • •

Serena and Jamar attended Finley High together since they were freshmen, but they rarely had cause to speak to each other. During their freshman year, Jamar was a quiet type, and he and Serena didn't have any classes together. Back then he was just another face in a large and usually rowdy crowd.

During her sophomore year, the two ended up in health class together, but Serena didn't think she spoke to him the entire time. Jamar was an introvert, and rumor had it he liked to read books that weren't assigned by any teacher. That type of behavior would've left him open to bullying from his peers, but Jamar was tall, and he looked like he might be able to defend himself.

His mother was Mexican, and his father was black. That left Jamar in the "biracial" category when it came to ethnicity. Fair skin was not really a big thing that year, so Jamar didn't get any special attention for his bronze complexion.

During her junior year, Serena began to notice Jamar a little more, but that was only because of a pretty girl he started to hang with. The girl was fair-skinned like him, and she had long hair that wasn't quite straight but definitely wasn't curly either. After a little investigating, Serena learned the pretty girl was Jamar's younger sister, Robyn.

Jamar was still a nobody, as far as Serena was concerned, when she started her senior year. But there were changes in both of their lives that ultimately caused their paths to intersect. On Jamar's side, he saw a void of religion at the school, and he took it upon himself to do something about it. He initially began to evangelize to some of his classmates, which caused rumors to spread around the school that he was a *weirdo*. But Jamar was not deterred by the criticism. In fact he doubled-down on his efforts.

The first time he and Serena officially spoke was in the cafeteria towards the end of lunch one day. She sat at a full table with her girlfriends. Her crew was often disorderly, and they didn't notice that Jamar had been making his way around the cafeteria, speaking to nearly everyone, until he approached them with an odd comment.

"Hi. Good afternoon. I was wondering if any of you young ladies would like to have a bible."

The immediate silence that fell upon their table was unnerving. Serena and her friends stared at Jamar like he'd lost his mind. She felt sorry for him when her friend Cicely cocked her head to the side and said, "*What you say?*" with enough attitude to make the school principal back down.

But Jamar didn't back down at all. He wore a collar shirt that was tucked into his jeans (even though that was not a dress code requirement) and a backpack (presumably stuffed with bibles) draped over his shoulder. He remained confident as he continued on his mission.

"Hi, my name's Jamar," he announced.

"We know who you is," Serena's other friend Toya snapped.

"Okay," Jamar said, still smiling pleasantly. "I was wondering if any of you ladies would like a free bible. I have some I'm giving away today."

"Why would we want a *bible*?" Cicely wanted to know.

"What are you, a Jehovah's Witness or something?" Toya asked.

At the time, Serena felt badly for Jamar, who had unwittingly walked into a den of female bullies. But she wasn't surprised by the way her girlfriends responded to him. Toya lived in the same projects as Serena, and everyone knew kids from the *jets* were not to be messed with. Jamar might as well have asked them if they'd like to accompany him to the library to do some extra credit work.

"I'm not a Jehovah's Witness," he said. "But I would like to spread the word about Jesus Christ. If any of you don't know Him, I can give you a bible, and we can talk about how He gave His life for you."

Jamar looked around the table and locked eyes with the girls one by one as he spoke. When he made eye contact with Serena, she had to look down at the leftover meal on her lunch tray. Jamar didn't seem to mind the reaction he was getting, but she was embarrassed for him.

"Ain't it illegal to talk about God at school?" Toya snapped.

"Maybe for the teachers, but not for us students," Jamar replied. He was very calm and collected.

"No, we don't want no damn *bibles*," Toya told him. "You stupid for asking people that."

Serena shook her head in disappointment. Did Toya ever have anything on her mind that didn't come out of her mouth? In addition to being needlessly rude, Toya was also the biggest gossip in the group.

"I don't think it's stupid," Jamar said. His smile was gone, but he didn't look upset. "Y'all have a nice day."

He walked away from their table, but he didn't go far. Serena watched as he approached the group behind them with the same request:

"Hi. Would any of you like a free bible?"

Cicely didn't wait until he was out of earshot before she rolled her eyes and said, "Why we got so many crazy people at our school?"

"It's crazy people at every school," the fourth member of their clique, Cassandra, replied.

"I know," Cicely said. "But I think we got *way* more retards over here."

"I know, right?" Toya said. She continued to give Jamar dirty looks, even though his back was to them now. "What's *wrong* with people?"

Serena wondered the same thing, but it wasn't just Jamar who was acting strange these days. Her boyfriend Cedric, known in the jets as *Lil C*, had been missing in action since Serena gave him all of herself on Valentine's Day and then again the following Saturday. The students at Finley High were now making preparations for spring break, and Cedric was like a ghost; a no-show at both school and in the neighborhood.

Serena wasn't worried about Cedric missing school, because his attendance had been spotty since the ninth grade. He had even told her that he would probably drop out for good one day. But Cedric's cellphone wasn't working anymore, and each time Serena went to his grandmother's house in search of him, the old woman said, "I ain't seen him."

Serena didn't know how that was possible. Cedric lived with his grandmother. He said she was his *legal guardian.* If he was in jail again – which wasn't totally out of the realm of possibilities – then his grandmother would know about it, wouldn't she? And if he went to live with someone else, Serena hoped his granny would tell her, rather than simply say, "I ain't seen him."

By the time March rolled around, Serena had an answer to one of her questions, and it was much more than she wanted to know. Thanks to an over-the-counter pregnancy test, she had solved the mystery of her missing period.

When she ran into Jamar again during passing period one day, her views on religion had changed. She had even begun to accompany her aunt to church on Sundays, which surprised and pleased Mary immensely.

Jamar approached Serena with a stack of fliers in hand that afternoon. Her friend Cicely spotted him first and tried to pull her away.

"Come on, girl. Here come that Jesus freak again."

But Serena stood her ground. "Hold up. I wanna see what he has to say."

"Why?" Cicely asked. "That boy is *strange*."

"He's alright," Serena told her. "Go ahead if you want to. I'll meet you outside."

Cicely gave her a peculiar look before fleeing the scene, and Serena loitered around her locker, waiting to see if Jamar had a flyer for her. After the way her friends had treated him in the cafeteria, she thought he would avoid her. But he didn't. He walked up to her like he didn't remember the previous encounter at all.

"Hi. I'm starting a bible club here at school. I was wondering if you'd like to join us."

He offered a postcard-size flyer that was very professional. The graphics were eye-catching, and it was double-sided. He started to walk away while Serena studied the flyer, but she stopped him.

"Wait."

He turned with a guarded expression. He remained a safe distance away from her, so Serena walked up to him.

"Why are you starting a bible club this late in the year?" she asked him. "School will be out in a couple of months."

A wave of relief washed over Jamar. It was clear he expected her to berate him, like her friends had done.

"God put it on my heart," he explained. "When God puts something on your heart, you have to be obedient, even if you think it might be too late."

Jamar wore a short-sleeved button-down with khakis that day. Finley High didn't have a strict dress code, so Serena was curious about why he chose to dress like a teacher. He kept his hair cut short on the sides. The hair on the top of his head was thick and wavy. He had a struggling mustache and a few stray hairs on his chin, but it wasn't enough to create a proper beard.

Jamar was a definite cutie, but his odd behavior at school tended to overshadow his good looks. As far as Serena knew, none of the girls at Finley High were interested in Jamar, not even the ugly ones.

"This is a nice flyer," she said. "Did you make it?"

Jamar smiled. Serena was surprised by how straight his teeth were. He never wore braces in high school, but surely he had in middle school.

"No. My dad made it for me."

"He works on computers?"

"Actually he's an engineer," Jamar told her. "Aeronautical. He works at Boeing. I don't think he designed this flyer personally, but he did get it designed and printed for me."

Serena had never met a black or Mexican student with an engineer in their family.

"You must be rich," she said.

33

"No, I'm poor," Jamar told her. "My dad tells me all the time: 'You don't have a job, and you don't have any income.' Everything I eat and wear is a donation from my parents. Without them, I'd be homeless."

Serena was surprised to hear such insight from a kid her age. She realized she was probably wrong for avoiding people like Jamar. Her friends never said anything insightful. In fact, it was her besties who thought she and Cedric would make a "*bomb couple.*"

"When is your bible club meeting?" she asked him.

Jamar's eyes lit up. Apparently this was the most interest anyone had shown thus far. "We're going to have our first meeting tomorrow," he told her. "After that, we'll meet twice a week in Mrs. Harding's classroom; at lunchtime on Mondays and Fridays."

"At lunchtime? How will y'all eat, if you're in a meeting?"

"I'll feed everyone who comes," Jamar assured her. "Tomorrow we're having pizza."

Serena was stunned. Pizza was a prized meal for high school students.

"You're going to bring pizza for everybody?"

He nodded. "Yes. I mean, no. I'm not bringing it from home. The principal says I can order it during third period. Are you going to come? If so, tell me what kind of pizza you like, and I'll make sure to get it."

"Oh, well I don't want to give you my order now," Serena said. "I might not come. I'll feel bad if you order it for me and I don't go."

"Don't worry about that. There's no pressure. I'm sure you're not the only person who likes whatever kind of pizza you want. What is it, pepperoni?"

She grinned and nodded.

"See, I was already gonna get that," Jamar told her. "So I'll see you tomorrow?"

She still didn't want to commit to it. "We'll see."

"Okay. I'll take that. What's your name?"

"Serena."

● ● ● ● ● ●

The next day she was too embarrassed to tell her friends where she was going at lunchtime, so Serena lied about having an upset stomach.

"I gotta find me a toilet," she told her cronies. "I think I got the runs."

"*Ewww. T.M.I,*" Toya said with a wrinkled up face. "Some things should be kept to yourself!"

When she got upstairs, Serena found the doorway to Mrs. Harding's classroom open, but she didn't hear any students talking inside. The reason for that became apparent when she walked in and saw Jamar sitting alone at one of the desks on the front row.

"Oh, I'm sorry. Am I too early?" Serena asked.

"No." Jamar shot to his feet. "You're right on time. You're the first person to get here."

"Oh, um..." She hesitated in the doorway. "Where's Mrs. Harding?"

"I'm just using her classroom," Jamar explained. "I don't know if she'll attend the meetings. She went out for lunch today. She said she can't eat pizza, because she's on a low-carb diet."

Serena frowned. She thought there would be at least ten students there, so she could blend in, preferably somewhere near the back. "I, um... I'll be back in a minute," she said as she backed out of the room.

"Wait, don't go," Jamar said. "Look. I got your pizza."

He gestured towards a table with ten pizza boxes stacked on it.

"You bought *all* of those pizzas?"

He nodded. "Three of them are pepperoni."

"Um..." Serena took another step back.

"Please don't go," Jamar pleaded. "I don't think anyone else is coming. I can't eat all of those by myself."

He looked so sweet and desperate, Serena couldn't help but smile.

"Come on," Jamar insisted. He reached and took hold of her hand. "Let's eat. We don't even have to talk about the bible today. We can talk about whatever you want to."

Serena was moved by his sincerity and his pitiful predicament. Plus Jamar was very handsome, in an unexpected kind of way. And Serena couldn't remember the last time a boy truly wanted her around – not for sex or anything like that. Just to talk. She took a deep breath and let it out with a soft sigh.

"Okay," she said and allowed him to pull her into the room.

● ● ● ● ● ●

Fifteen minutes later they were still the only ones there, and they had only managed to eat one of Jamar's pizzas – well, most of it anyway. Surprisingly, Serena found his company refreshing. Jamar wasn't like any of the other students at the school. He was smart and sensitive, a real thinker. And even in the midst of failure, he remained confident about his cause. He kept his word about them not discussing the bible that day, but he did want to know about Serena's change of heart.

"I'm surprised you came," he told her. "You and your friends didn't seem interested in stuff like this when I talked to you in the cafeteria that time…"

Serena's face burned with embarrassment. "I'm sorry about that. It doesn't take much to get them turned-up. But it wasn't me. I didn't say anything to you that day."

The two of them sat facing each other on either side of a small table. The classroom door was open, but the hallways were quiet and deserted. So far Serena's time with Jamar had been cozy and disarming. She was actually glad no one else bothered to show up to his bible club meeting.

"I noticed you didn't hop on the bandwagon with your friends," he said. "I thought that was kinda cool."

The praise was insignificant, but it warmed Serena's heart nonetheless.

"Do people talk to you that way a lot?" she wondered. "Like the way my friends did?"

"Are those really your friends?" Jamar asked.

Serena was confused by the question. "Yeah. Why do you say that?"

He shrugged. "I don't know. If I was hanging around people who treated someone badly, and I didn't agree with it, I would stop hanging around those people."

Serena thought that was such a *parent* thing to say – well, maybe a responsible parent would say stuff like that. To her recollection, her mom never objected to anyone Serena hung out with. And some of her friends were real-life hoodlums.

She asked another question, rather than respond to his. "How do you handle it, when people make fun of you?"

"It depends," Jamar said. "If it's someone I care about, like a cousin or a good friend, I'll tell them what I don't like about it and ask them to stop. If it's a stranger, who I'll probably never talk to again, I won't say anything. What do I care what some stranger thinks about me?"

Serena nodded. She wished she was as self-assured as he was.

"But why do you do it?" she asked. "You know most kids at school don't care about God and stuff..."

"That's exactly why I do it," Jamar said, his eyes brightening. "The same students who don't care about Jesus probably don't know that He can change their life. There are a lot of people at this school who are suffering. They're battling depression, gangs, drugs – you name it. They don't know that the devil has a foothold in their lives, and they have the power to defeat him. They don't even know they're in a spiritual war."

"But why *you*?" Serena pressed. "Why do you think you have to be the one to tell them?"

Jamar shrugged. "Instead of asking myself why I should do something, I'd rather ask myself *why not*. If I know the right thing to do, but I choose not to do it, that's a sin. I don't think I could sleep at night, if I went home every day knowing I didn't even *try* to help people. I saw them hurting, but I didn't even try..."

Serena knew she wasn't going to get a better answer out of him. People like Jamar didn't care about what others thought about them, as long as they were doing what they knew was right. It was rare to find someone in high school who was so selfless, so righteous.

"Is there something going on in your life that brought you to this meeting?" he asked.

Their conversation had been going so smoothly, Serena almost told him. But she held back. According to her guesstimates, she was about two months pregnant at the time. There were only a couple of months left in school, so it was possible to make it all the way to graduation before her belly size revealed the secret about the life she was nurturing.

One of Serena's main goals had always been to graduate high school without having a baby. Technically she would accomplish that. It was probably childish thinking, but her new goal was to make it to graduation without anyone knowing she was pregnant. And yes, that included her mom. So far Serena had only told one person. She was positive her best friend wouldn't tell anyone else.

After a noticeable pause, Jamar said, "It's cool if you don't want to talk about it. I know you don't know me that well."

"I don't know you at all," she confirmed.

"Yeah. But I hope we can get to know each other better..."

If anyone else said that to her, Serena would've considered it flirting. But she knew that Jamar's heart was pure and so were his words. It wouldn't surprise her if he was still a virgin.

"I hope you'll come to our next meeting," he said when she didn't respond.

She said, "I might."

He checked the clock hanging on the wall over the dry erase board. Serena looked too. She was surprised that their lunch break was about to end. It didn't feel like forty whole minutes had passed.

"Do you want to take some pizza home?" he asked her.

Serena's eyes brightened, but they dulled just as quickly. She could imagine the smiles on her brother and sisters' faces if she came home with all of that pizza. She considered her family to be relatively poor. Not *soup-kitchen poor*, but poorer than most of the other kids at her school.

Her mother Princess had a debit card from welfare, but they could only buy food from the store with that. A fast-food burger was somewhat of a delicacy in their household. A pizza was even better, and Jamar had nine of them!

"I do want to take one, but I walk home," she told him. "It's too far to walk with a pizza."

"Where do you live?" he asked. "I can get my mom to drop you off after school. You can take all of these pizzas, if you want…"

Serena frowned at that. She'd go to sleep tonight with no supper at all before she allowed him to treat her like a charity case.

"No. That's alright."

Before Jamar could insist, the bell rang, bringing their time together to an end. Serena shot to her feet, suddenly eager to be away from him. Jamar stood as well.

"Wait. Don't forget that we meet every Monday and Friday, right here."

"Who is this *we* you're talking about?" she joked. "You're the only member of your bible club."

"Yeah, but if you join, then there will be *two* members," he said with a bright smile. "Two's better than one. And four is better than two. Rome wasn't built in a day."

Serena couldn't help but return his smile. "We'll see."

She walked out of the classroom and quickly disappeared among the crowd of students who packed the hallways after each period.

CHAPTER FOUR
AN UNEXPECTED REQUEST

Over the next few weeks, Serena did continue to attend Jamar's meetings, and thankfully she wasn't the only one. By the end of April, there were at least eight other students who became official members of the bible club. Sometimes they got even more attendees from curious folks and hungry kids who heard Jamar was offering free food.

Serena complained about these *opportunists* from time to time, but Jamar told her it didn't matter what brought people to God, so long as they did get to know Him at some point. Even Mrs. Harding stopped leaving the campus for lunch, and she became the first adult member of the group.

Of course getting away from her friends at lunchtime twice a week proved to be a challenge for Serena. Eventually she told them where she was going, and she stood tall in the face of their criticism.

"*Bible club?*" Toya's face was scrunched up, as if Serena told her she had joined the school's chess team.

"Why you wanna do that?" her friend Cassandra asked.

"Why not?" Serena shot back. "What's wrong with the bible?"

"Nothing's wrong with it," Toya said. "But that's what they got *church* for. Why you wanna talk about God at school?"

Serena shrugged. "It's better than all of the other crap we talk about. We can talk about who's fighting who and who's sexing who, but we can't talk about God?"

"That's lame," Toya said with a roll of her eyes.

"You like that boy, Jamar?" Cicely guessed.

Serena frowned and shook her head. "No. He's just my friend."

"Y'all been hanging out a lot lately," Cicely noticed.

Jamar had been approaching Serena a lot more these days, but she didn't think anything of it. She figured they'd developed some sort of comradery because she was the first member of his club. She certainly didn't think he was attracted to her, or anything like that.

"Don't you go with Lil C?" Toya asked her.

Serena smacked her lips. "He *been* gone. I don't even know where he lives anymore. But I don't like Jamar, either. We're just friends."

"Tell me you're only going to those meetings for the free food," Cassandra said.

"For real," Toya agreed. "That's the only reason I would go. But I wouldn't even be able to fake it for that long. I'd probably just grab my pizza and leave before he started talking about whatever the hell y'all be talking about in there. That boy is *weird*."

Serena hated to hear her friends speaking negatively about Jamar, but she wasn't surprised. In fact, Jamar told her this would happen when her crew realized she was going to the meetings. He said people who followed Jesus had been ostracized and persecuted since Christianity was founded, and that was something that would never change.

Serena considered defending Jamar; insisting that he wasn't a weirdo, and compared to him, her friends were the ones who were lost, stupid and *weird*. But they would assume that she did have feelings for him if she said that.

"Look, I got stuff going on in my life that can be really depressing, if I think about it long enough," she said sincerely. "Y'all can't help me, and my mama can't help me, and Jamar can't help me, either. At this point, God is the only one who can help me. So don't get mad at me because I want to get right with Him."

Serena turned and walked away from her friends with tears in her eyes. Cicely was the only one who knew about the pregnancy, so she hurried to catch up with her.

"Wait. Where you going?"

It was lunchtime on a Thursday. Serena wished Jamar's meetings were five days a week rather than two, because she actually had nowhere to run to.

"I don't know," she said. She slowed down so her friend could walk with her.tside, I guess."

"It's okay if you want to go to those meetings," Cicely told her.

"Thanks, but I don't need your permission," Serena snapped.

"I'm just saying," Cicely went on, "if you tell them what's going on with you, they'll understand too."

"I shouldn't have to tell them my life is jacked up," Serena countered. "There's nothing wrong with me going to some stupid meetings. I don't owe them an explanation."

"Yeah, but you know they retarded," Cicely said. She smiled, and Serena did, too.

"Don't say that," she said. "That's actually an insult to *real* retarded people."

● ● ● ● ● ●

After denying that Jamar had any interest in her outside of the bible club, Serena couldn't have been more surprised when he stopped by her locker after school with beads of sweat on his forehead.

"Hey. Uh, hi," he said.

Serena's eyes narrowed in confusion. Jamar wasn't the coolest cat in the game – far from it – but he wasn't shy at all, at least not that she had ever seen.

"Hi," she said. "What's up?"

"I, um..." He looked down at his sneakers. "This is gonna sound really stupid..."

Serena became more intrigued. She looked down at his shoes too, thinking his apprehension might have something to do with his Converse.

"What's gonna sound really stupid?"

He looked up at her, and she noticed the sweat on his brow.

"Is everything alright?" she asked.

"Yes," he said. "Well, no. The thing is, I've never done anything like this before, and I, I don't know how. I'm starting to feel like this is a bad idea. I should go."

45

He started to walk away. Serena reached and touched his shoulder.

"Wait, Jamar. You can't just leave like that. Now I'm curious about what you wanted..."

He turned and took a deep breath. He looked around and noticed a poster announcing the school prom taped next to Serena's locker.

"It's *that*," he said, his eyes glued to the poster.

Serena turned and stared at it, too. Her eyes were wide, her heart fluttering, when she returned her attention to Jamar.

"I'm not going," he said. "Well, I never planned on going. It's no big deal. You know? I've never been on a date, and I haven't gone to any school dances. I can't dance, and I don't have a girlfriend. So, you know, stuff like that isn't for me."

Serena didn't know any of that, but she could've guessed it was the case. But why was he sharing all of this with her? She remained silent, hoping he would continue to divulge.

"But I was talking to my mom," he said, "because she was making plans for my sister to go to the prom this year. You know my sister is younger than me. She's a junior. Her boyfriend is a senior, and he invited her, so she's going. So my mom asked me why I wasn't going, and I told her, you know, everything I just told you. And she says I should go because the prom is supposed to be some kind of once in a lifetime experience."

He shrugged. "I don't know about all of that, but I do know that everybody makes a big deal about it, and my mom says that for a senior, it's almost as important as graduation. And I haven't seen you with any boys at school, so I don't

46

know if, you know, if you were going with somebody or not. But I know you probably are, because, you know, you're real pretty and stuff.

"But if there was some chance that you weren't going with somebody already, and you do want to go, but you don't have anyone to go with, then I figured maybe you would go with me – *as friends* – and I can buy the tickets for you. For us. I can get our tickets."

He was going a mile a minute. He took a deep breath when he finished his spiel and wiped the perspiration from his forehead. After he wiped it, he looked at the back of his hand and was surprised to see so much sweat.

"Oh, Jesus," he muttered. "I am really nervous. Sorry. I promise I don't usually sweat like this."

Serena was surprised, confused, reluctant and excited, all at the same time. Like Jamar, she had already decided the senior prom was something that would pass her by. She wanted to go, had dreamed about it for over a year. But after her boyfriend left her high and dry with a bun in the oven, she figured the prom was one of many childish aspirations that were no longer for her.

But it didn't have to be that way. Jamar was probably the *last* person she would consider an ideal prom date, but that didn't have to be the case, either. In fact, Jamar was probably the safest boy she could go to the prom with. They got along just fine, and he was definitely good-looking. Plus she knew he wouldn't try to pressure her for sex, drugs or even a goodnight kiss.

Serena considered whether it would be right for her to attend the prom now that she was with child, but she would only be three months pregnant on prom night. She wasn't showing now, and she doubted if she'd have a baby bulge in just two weeks.

And Jamar said they would only be going *as friends*, so she didn't feel obligated to tell him about her condition. If he wanted to go out on a real date, that would be different. But she wasn't required to tell a *friend* anything.

"You want to go to the prom with me?" she asked.

Jamar was wary. He hoped she wasn't setting him up for a cruel rejection.

"Yes. If you're not going with someone already, I think we would have fun."

Serena smiled, which replaced the heat he was feeling with a cool, summer rain.

"Okay," she said. "That would be nice."

Jamar couldn't believe it. His heart became so light, he thought it might float right out of his chest.

"*Really?*"

"Yes," Serena said with a giggle. "As *friends*, right?"

"Oh. Yes. Of course. *As friends.*"

"Then yes," she said. "I would love to go with you."

Jamar's delight seemed to belie the fact that he only liked her as a friend, but Serena didn't call him on it. If he never asked a girl out on a date, then even this friendly one would be a big deal to him.

"Okay. Great," he said. "I'll order the tickets tomorrow." His smile was ear to ear. "Let me know when you get your dress, so I can make sure to get a cummerbund that matches it. My mom says that's a big deal, too."

Serena's heart froze at the mention of her prom dress, but she kept her smile glued in place. Two minutes ago her life was just fine without the prom. But now that she actually had a date, she wouldn't let anything stop her from attending. Come hell or high water, she would find a way to get a prom dress. She didn't think her incarcerated father could offer any assistance, but she would even write a letter begging him for help.

● ● ● ● ● ●

Over the next week her friendship with Jamar seemed to change, but Serena was reluctant to admit that she noticed. The time they spent together at the bible club meetings was the same. It was their interactions outside of those meetings that were different. Jamar walked her to her classes each time he ran into her during passing period, and he always showed up at her locker after school.

Serena's girlfriends were quick to point out the fact that she appeared to be in a relationship with "*Bible Boy*," but she shot that down every time she heard it.

"We're just friends," she insisted. "I would never go out with someone like Jamar."

"But you're going to the prom with him," Toya countered.

"Only *as friends*," Serena said. "Neither one of us had anyone to go with, so we decided to go together. It's no big deal."

"I don't know," Cassandra told her. "I seen the way he looks at you. I think he wants to be more than friends."

Serena wondered about that as well, but she would deny it with her dying breath. If she and Jamar were in a *relationship*, then she'd be obligated to tell him she was pregnant – at which point he would dump her and certainly not take her to the prom.

"What would I look like going with somebody like Jamar?" she asked her friends. "That boy is a *virgin*. I'd date a freshman, before I'd date him."

Her friends laughed at that, and Serena silently cursed herself for throwing Jamar under the bus. She thought about what the bible club discussed last week: Jamar had warned them about friends who require you to act a certain way around them – a way that goes against who you really are on the inside.

Serena knew this was exactly the kind of thing he was referring to, but she found herself stuck between a rock and a hard place. She and Cicely and Toya and Cassandra had been friends since the sixth grade. These *fast girls* were her *clique*. Maybe Serena did feel differently about some things as of late, but she didn't think it was enough to throw away seven years of friendship.

● ● ● ● ● ●

Serena told *most* of this to her aunt as they drove from the mall with her prom dress in the back seat. She did not tell her aunt about the pregnancy or about bad-mouthing Jamar or about her fears that their "just friends" scenario was starting to feel a little iffy.

When she was done talking, Aunt Mary took a few moments to absorb the information before saying, "Jamar sounds like an awesome young man. Are you sure he doesn't like you a little more than you like him?"

"We're just friends," Serena said, for what felt like the thousandth time.

"Okay," Mary said. She decided to let it go, though it was clear she had more thoughts on the subject. "What about your interest in the bible club?" she asked. "It sounds like you started going to those meetings around the same time you started coming to church with me..."

That wasn't a question, so Serena remained mute. Aunt Mary had been trying to figure out her niece's sudden interest in religion for a few weeks now. So far Serena would only tell her, "I just wanna go to church. Do I have to have a reason?"

Mary would tell her, "No, you don't have to have a reason," and they would leave it at that. But the story about Jamar's bible club piqued her interest again. Mary feared that her niece had been through some traumatic experience. Serena wasn't physically wounded, so it would have to be something emotionally traumatic. Or maybe she was in the midst of a life or death dilemma right now. Mary couldn't understand how something like that could be happening right under their noses, but her sister Princess wasn't the most observant mother.

Mary had been waiting and hoping Serena would come clean. Surely the girl knew that she could count on her aunt for anything at this point. Or could it be Serena was being honest, and there was nothing bad going on in her life? Once again she decided to let it go. Regardless of the reason Serena ran to God, she was glad her niece made the move. And if there was some dark secret involved, Mary was confident it would eventually come to light.

"What about your shoes?" she asked. "Do you want to wear pumps or heels?"

"Oh no," Serena said, already on the verge of another financial meltdown. "I forgot about shoes. I don't have any money left."

"Don't worry," Mary said with a grin. "We can stop by my house after church tomorrow to see if I have anything you like. If not, I'll take you to Payless."

"Thanks," Serena said with a smile.

Another crisis averted. She never considered herself lucky before, but when it came to this prom, everything seemed to be falling into place for her. If it wasn't for the fact that her life would go down the toilet shortly after graduation, Serena might be foolish enough to think she was finally on the right track.

CHAPTER FIVE
PRINCESS AND THE JETS

It was late in the afternoon when Aunt Mary exited the freeway and turned onto Chambers Street; the major thoroughfare in Serena's neighborhood. There were over a hundred identical red brick buildings in the Powell Housing Projects, which were casually known as the jets.

Serena didn't know why the low-income development was called the *projects* or why the word had been shortened to the *jets*. She wondered if *project* meant her neighborhood was some sort of social experiment, like a science project. If that was the case, the experiment had failed miserably.

Not only did all of the apartments look alike, but the people inside the stale, brick walls were the same too. Almost every unit had more kids than their mother could afford to care for and no married couple working hard to raise them.

There were plenty of men around. But rather than take the responsibility that came with the *husband* label, they preferred other titles, like *boyfriend, baby-daddy, sugar daddy, sex buddy* or *Mama's Friend Who Spends the Night Sometimes.*

These unsavory conditions combined to create an environment that was flush with laziness and misery, which brought alcohol and drugs, which catered to thieves and dealers. The end result of this drama was always the same: Black men went to prison for decades at a time, if they were lucky. The unlucky ones got transferred to a new housing project in the cemetery.

The female residents in Serena's neighborhood fared a little better, meaning they didn't get killed as often. But they were still trapped in a cycle of doom that was hard to escape. Typically they didn't get a good education, and they had children young and out of wedlock. By the time they reached adulthood, these girls were mirror images of their mothers.

Serena thought she was on track to break this cycle, but the life growing inside her womb was proof that she was just another statistic. She tried not to think about it when her aunt pulled to a stop in front of her building. Serena exited the vehicle with her prom dress cradled in her arms.

"Thanks again, for everything," she said before she closed the passenger door.

"It's fine, Serena," Aunt Mary said. "I'll come by in the morning to pick you up for church."

"Thanks, Auntie."

"You're gonna be the prettiest girl at the prom," Mary predicted. "I'm so excited for you."

"Me too," Serena said. Her smile was bright and innocent.

When she entered her home, Serena was greeted by three crumb-snatchers before she even had time to take her dress to her bedroom. Her sister Sheila and her brother Paul looked like they hadn't been doing anything the whole time Serena was gone. They were on the couch watching TV when she left, and they were still in this position. They left their seats and rushed to her, like she was their father returning home from a long, hard day at work.

"Serena! *Ooh! Let me see!*"

Sheila was eight years old. She was a boney girl with big teeth, fair skin and unkempt hair that typically only got styled on school days.

"Dang. Where'd you get that?" her brother asked.

Paul was twelve and very mature for his age. He was a little *too* mature, as far as Serena was concerned, but she knew that was something that came with the territory. The girls in the neighborhood could avoid the gangs and dealers who were always clamoring around them. But the young boys had to toughen-up quickly, if they wanted to do the same.

Serena was adamant about Paul not getting involved in the criminal element in the projects. So far he'd been successful in remaining autonomous, but occasionally he had to fight to remain that way. Sometimes Serena had to track down Paul's tormentors and fight for him. As far as she was concerned, that's what families were for.

Her third sibling, Annette (more commonly known as Annie), was only six months old. She climbed off the couch and crawled to greet her big sister as well.

Serena would never forget the way she reacted when her mother told her she was pregnant again with Annie. She was only a child herself, but at that point Serena was old enough to know that another child would make their meager living conditions in the projects even worse.

"Why, Mama?" she had cried, her eyes thick with tears.

"What do you mean *why*?" Princess had said.

"Why you having another baby?" Serena asked. "It's already hard enough here as it is."

That was last year. Serena was seventeen at the time. Princess couldn't believe her own daughter was trying to put her in check.

She told her, "I didn't plan it, Serena. Damn. It's not like I *wanted* to have another baby."

"*But you didn't have to get pregnant!*" Serena had bawled. "Why didn't you use a condom? Why you don't have your tubes tied?"

That comment made Princess' eyes widen, and anger began to replace the surprise of her daughter being so worldly.

"I'm the one having a baby – not you!" Princess growled. "I don't see why you so worried about it anyway."

"Because *I'm* the one who gotta take care of him," Serena said knowingly. She knew this because the pattern had been in place for years. Her daily household duties went so far past babysitting, Serena thought she could be considered at least a *secondary* guardian for her siblings.

"Ain't nobody asked you to do *nothing*!" Princess shouted before heading to her bedroom. "Even if I do ask you to help out sometimes, ain't nothing wrong with that, Serena. We're a *family*, and we all help each other. You ain't special."

Serena smiled as she looked down at her sister and thought back to that stressful day. Annie wore a pink onesie with a big diaper bulge beneath it. The baby had bright eyes and a smile that could light up any gloomy day. Her life may have begun as an unplanned pregnancy, but she was now a precious life that no one in the house could live without.

"Hey, *snookie pookie*," Serena cooed as she looked down at her.

The baby gurgled something that sounded like, "Mama."

"Let me see your dress!" Sheila demanded.

Serena was now in the center of a tight circle of love. She smiled as she held the dress up by the hanger and removed the clear bag that covered it. The prom dress seemed to glow under the 60 watt bulbs they had in the living room. The purple waistband was dazzling. The dress was immediately the most cherished and possibly the most expensive item in the home.

"*Wow*," Sheila said, her eyes wide, her mouth ajar.

Even Paul, who generally could care less about girlie things, stared at the dress in awe.

"How you get the money for that?" he asked.

Before Serena could respond, her mother entered the room wearing the khakis and golf shirt required for her new job at Safeway. Princess quickly took in the scene, and, not surprisingly, she had the same question as Paul.

"Girl, where you get the money for that dress? Mary bought it for you?"

Princess Rupp was 35 years old. She had Serena when she was seventeen. She was brown-skinned and reasonably attractive with big boobs, big hips and a big butt that attracted way too much attention.

When she was younger, Serena often contemplated the irony of her mother's name. Princess was like none of the princesses in the storybooks Serena used to read. She was married once, but that relationship was no fairy tale.

Serena's father was a drug dealer, and sometimes he robbed people too. He got arrested when Serena was a toddler, and he was still caged-up like an animal.

After Big Pat, Princess had a string of relationships with frogs who did not turn into princes when she kissed them. But she had three more babies with those frogs anyway. The end result of her sexual escapades was a single mother of four who worked sparingly and accepted state and government assistance in copious amounts.

Serena would never go as far as to say her mother was a *disappointment*, but she rarely had cause to say she was proud of her, either. She had a sinking feeling in her gut as Princess approached to get a better look at the dress.

"Daddy bought it for me," she said, almost meekly.

Princess' pudgy features morphed into a deep frown. "Your daddy? *Pat?*"

That's the only dad I got, Serena almost told her, but she knew smart-aleck answers like that didn't play well in her house. Princess wasn't the type of mom to beat her kids regularly, but blatant disrespect might earn you a swift backhand, depending on her mood.

"Yes," she said.

Princess' head tilted slowly to the side as she looked up from the dress and met her daughter's eyes.

Serena thought her mom was a little chubby but still pretty, even though her attitude made her look ugly sometimes.

"How the hell Pat buy a dress for you?" she wanted to know.

Serena didn't notice, but her brother and sisters all quieted down and backed away slowly when their mother

KEITH THOMAS WALKER

raised her voice; similar to the way a pack of wolves responds to the angry alpha male.

"Aunt Mary went to visit him, and he gave her the money," Serena explained.

"Where he get money from?" her mother asked.

Serena shrugged. "I don't know. Aunt Mary say he probably still hustling."

Princess accepted that easily enough. If there was one thing her ex-husband was good at, it was buying for cheap and selling at a profit, aka hustling.

"She went to see him?"

"Yeah," Serena said, wondering why her mother didn't visit her ex-husband more often herself. "Auntie said he put the money in a bag of chips and gave it to her."

"Hmph," Princess said. She took a step back and rested a hand on her hip. "How much he give you?"

Serena knew the answer would bring more drama, but there was no point in lying about something that was so easily verifiable. Aunt Mary may have been a co-conspirator, but she wouldn't keep the truth from Princess if she asked her.

"Three hundred dollars," she said softly.

"*Three hundred dollars*?!" Princess went from zero to one hundred in the blink of an eye. "Girl, you know what we could've did what that money? We got bills due *right now*! Why he give it to you? Why he didn't give it to me? I'm the one taking care of your butt!"

Because he knew you'd waste it at the club, Serena thought, but again she didn't say it out loud.

Princess' club-hopping was a huge source of contention in their household. Serena didn't like to babysit when her mother went out partying, which happened at least twice a month. Serena was even less pleased about the unsuitable men Princess sometimes brought home with her.

Princess would try to be discreet about her bedroom activities, for the most part. But at some point her dates would have to leave or go to the bathroom, at which point they would inevitably run into one of her four kids.

But Serena actually preferred that her mother come home every night, even if it was with a new boyfriend. The alternative meant she had to spend the night at some unknown location with some strange man, which would lead to her children worrying about her safety all night long.

"I didn't know you needed it," Serena offered.

"*Yes you did*!" her mother countered. "Girl, you see how we living in here. How you figure we don't need no money? Don't nobody in this house got a stitch of clothes that cost three hundred dollars. What makes you think you should have a dress like that?"

The dress was actually $374 after taxes, but Serena definitely didn't volunteer that information.

"You only gon' wear it *one time*," Princess continued to rant. "And a prom ain't that dang important! You could care less about it a month ago. Now it's all you can think about. I know you think you all in love with that boy who's taking you—"

"I don't love him. We're just friends."

"You think that's supposed to make it better? It actually makes it *worse*, Serena! You just spent a lot of money for a dress you're going to wear *one time* at a party that only lasts a couple of hours, and you're going with somebody who ain't even your boyfriend. You know what that means?"

Serena knew her mother was going to call her *stupid*, but Princess had a new insult today.

"You *selfish*, Serena! You ain't thinking about nobody but yourself. I could'a took a day off today, if I had three hundred dollars..."

Serena was on the verge of giving this argument a little credence until her mother said that. She could've taken a day off? Princess had only been working at her current job for a couple of months. Granted, being a grocery store cashier wasn't a career Princess was especially proud of, but it was a job. It brought the household much needed income. The fact that she would skip her shift at Safeway today if she suddenly had a pocketful of money said a lot about Princess' work ethics and her overall competence as a provider.

But I'm the selfish one, Mama? Really?

But none of this was new to Serena, nor was it particularly shocking, so she kept her mouth shut and absorbed the verbal abuse like she always did. Luckily Princess was done for now. She turned and retreated to her bedroom, leaving her four children in a state of shock and silence.

After a moment, Serena went to the room she shared with Sheila and hung her dress in the closet. All of her siblings followed her, because even at a young age they knew that there was strength in numbers. Plus Serena had always been a smarter and gentler mother duck to the string of vulnerable ducklings.

CHAPTER SIX
MAMA-SISTER

Twenty minutes later Princess left for work, and the tension in the house left with her. Sheila was the first one to try to recapture the lighthearted atmosphere they had before their mother went off on one of her tirades.

"Can you put your dress on, so I can see it?"

Serena smiled and was happy to oblige.

The dress fit her as well as it did in the department store, except it wasn't as tight around the stomach this time. Serena guessed that was because she hadn't eaten since noon, which was nearly six hours ago. She modeled the dress for her brother and sisters, before she headed to the kitchen to find something to cook for dinner.

All four kids crowded the bathroom as Serena checked out her physique in the mirror. She might have been a little pregnant, but for now she was still fine. She had a slim waist that blossomed into nice, child-bearing hips like her mom. Her skin was honey brown. Her lips nice and plump. The dress only revealed about an inch of cleavage, which Serena thought was a perfect amount.

Jamar didn't seem like the type of guy who would appreciate all of her sexiness, but Serena thought he'd have to be blind not to feel *something* when he saw her in this dress.

Her mother made her feel like Cinderella sometimes, with all of the yelling and a never-ending list of household chores. On prom night, Serena would dress up in her expensive dress and ride a carriage that was magically transformed from a pumpkin. That thought made her giggle as she stared at her reflection.

"You so pretty," Sheila said as she leaned over the sink. "I hope I look like you when I get big."

"You only need to worry about one thing when you get big," Serena warned her.

"I know," Sheila said with a roll of her eyes. "No babies before I graduate."

"That's right," Serena told her. "You too," she said to her little brother.

Paul smacked his lips. "Man, I can't even have no babies."

"Oh yes you can," Serena said. "You keep running around thinking like that, and you gon' have a whole room full of 'em!"

● ● ● ● ● ●

Serena found a pound of ground beef in the fridge, which opened up a world of opportunities, as far as dinner was concerned. They didn't have any lettuce or tomatoes, so Paul's request for a cheeseburger was crossed off the list.

"We don't even have any cheese," Serena complained.

"Didn't Mama leave you a debit card?" Paul asked.

All three of Serena's siblings lurked on the outskirts of the kitchen, because she didn't like them in the area when she was trying to cook.

"They don't sell lettuce and tomatoes at the corner store," she told her brother.

"They sell cheese," Sheila offered.

"We can go to Kroger's," Paul suggested.

Serena shook her head at that. Kroger's was the closest real grocery store. It was located on Chambers Street but not within the housing projects. The two mile walk wasn't a problem on some days, but now it was near sunset. Serena would have to go by herself and leave her brother and sisters alone, or she'd have to take everyone and make a family trip out of it.

"I'm not going nowhere with Annie at this time of day," she quickly decided.

There hadn't been a shooting in the projects for over a month, but that only meant they were probably due for another one. And everyone knows bullets don't have anyone's name on them.

Serena went to the cabinet and found a knock-off Hamburger Helper meal.

"Looks like we're eating cheesy mac," she announced.

That brought a "Yay!" from Sheila and a disappointed "Aww, man," from Paul.

"We always eating *macaroni*," he complained.

Serena looked back and saw a heavy frown pulling his lips down.

"Hamburger Helper isn't macaroni."

"Same thing," he said. "The noodles look just like macaroni. And that's not even a real Hamburger Helper.

Can't you just make me a hamburger? I'll eat it without cheese."

"We don't have anything to put on it, except for bread," Serena explained.

"That's fine with me," Paul pouted.

"I'm not doing that," Serena said. "You gotta eat what everybody else eats."

"I'm going to see what Sammy and them got to eat," Paul said and headed for the front door.

"You can't go outside now!" Serena called. "It's too late."

"No it's not."

"It's dark outside."

"The streetlights haven't came on yet," the boy protested.

"I don't care if they on or not," Serena shouted. "They're probably broke. I said it's too late to go outside, and that's it! If you take a foot outside this house, I'ma chase you down and beat your butt – right in front of *Sammy and them.*"

At twelve years of age Paul was always eager to assert his manliness, but tussling with his big sister was never a good idea. He knew that she would follow through with her threat and whoop him in front of his friends, just to make a point.

"Man, I hate it here," Paul whined as he plopped down on the living room couch to wait for his supper.

● ● ● ● ● ●

Dinner was ready twenty minutes later. It turned out to be a really good meal. Even Paul, who supposedly hated macaroni, cleaned his bowl and asked for seconds. Serena didn't have any more left, but she didn't tell him that. She took his and her bowl to the kitchen and gave him the rest of her meal.

A moment later Serena remembered that she was pregnant, and in lieu of the prenatal exams she should be getting, the least she could do was keep the baby healthy by eating for two. She made herself a bologna sandwich and ate it quickly in the kitchen before Paul realized she made a sacrifice for him.

Serena heard the house phone ringing while she was bottle-feeding Annie in her bedroom. A few seconds later Sheila appeared in the doorway with the cordless phone in hand.

"Telephone," she announced with a slick grin. "It's your *boyfriend*."

Serena frowned. She hadn't heard from her boyfriend in nearly two months. Cedric wasn't even her boyfriend anymore, as far as she was concerned. But Serena was eager to tell him about the child she would soon bring into the world. She also wanted to confront him about taking off his condom and getting her pregnant in the first place.

But when she grabbed the phone, it was Jamar on the other end, not Cedric. Serena's aggravation quickly dissipated as she returned to her spot on the bed with Annie in her arms and the phone propped between her ear and shoulder.

"Hey, what you doing?"

"Just got back from ordering my tux," Jamar said.

She could hear his excitement over the phone, which made a smile brighten her features as well.

"You got it already? I just told you what color my dress is a few hours ago."

"My mom wanted to make sure they'd have my size in stock," Jamar explained. "Plus the prom is only a week away. She doesn't like to wait till the last minute to do anything."

"You brought the tux home?"

"No. I'll pick it up next Friday. I made sure to get a *wine berry purple* cummerbund. The lady didn't look funny when I told her the color, so I guess it's something people ask for all the time."

"That's awesome. I can't wait to see you in your tux."

"And I can't wait to see you in your dress!"

His comment warmed Serena's heart, even though it could be considered flirtatious. She knew their situation was a little *different*, and it was getting more complicated by the day. Jamar never flat out complimented her, but sometimes he did, in a roundabout way, like the time he said her pink lipstick reminded him of bubblegum.

On that day, he stared at her mouth for so long Serena felt like he wanted to kiss her. And she wanted to kiss him, too. But that kiss would cross the line, on so many levels. Even though Serena was going to church now, she still felt like a big-time sinner. Jamar, on the other hand, was very holy-holy.

"I was wondering what you wanted to do after the prom," he said.

Serena hadn't given it much thought. "I don't know. I don't think people do anything special, except go to parties and stuff. But I'm sure you wouldn't want to go to any of those. I heard they be doing a lot of drinking and stuff."

The *stuff* Serena was referring to was a bunch of premarital sex, another thing she was certain Jamar was opposed to.

"I don't mind going to a party, if you want to," he said. "Prom is supposed to be special. I don't want you to feel like you missed out on anything, just because you went with me."

"It'll still be special if we don't go to a party," she assured him. "Don't forget, I wasn't gonna go at all until you asked me. Just being there will be special enough. I won't be comfortable around a bunch of kids drinking."

"Oh, okay," Jamar said. "But we should find *something* to do after it's over. I don't want to take you home early, while everyone else is still out having fun."

"Don't worry about everybody else, Jamar. That's how people give in to peer pressure; trying to be like the other kids."

He chuckled. "You sound like my mom. She told me the same thing today, when were out looking for my tux."

"Then you should listen to her. I don't need anything else, but to go to the prom with you."

Serena caught herself the moment she finished the sentence. *Dang it.* It was getting harder and harder to talk to Jamar without progressing their relationship – *friendship* that is. She didn't want to lead him on, because there was no way they could be together. The moment she told him she was pregnant, he'd be out of her life.

And that was for the best. Jamar was a good kid. He was going to college, where he'd fall in love with a virgin, just like him, and they'd wait until they got married before they had sex for the first time. Serena knew that she was already damaged goods. She was a pregnant hood rat, like her mother was at her age.

"That's all I need, too," Jamar said. "Just to be with you."

Serena's heart began to thud. Her breaths became heated. There was absolutely nothing she could do with that comment except ignore it.

She looked down at Annie and saw that the baby was no longer sucking her bottle. Her eyes were closed, and she was drifting off to sleep. Serena propped her up on her shoulder to burp her before she took her to the crib. The baby belched loudly after a few pats on the back.

"*Eww*. You nasty," Jamar said.

"Boy, that wasn't me," Serena replied with a laugh. "I just burped my little sister."

"Oh, I didn't know you had the baby. She's so quiet."

"I was feeding her. Now I'm done. I'm about to take her to her crib."

"That's awesome, how you take care of her," Jamar said. "You're going to make a great mother one day."

Yeah, one day real soon, Serena thought, and her eyes unexpectedly filled with tears.

CHAPTER SEVEN
VOICE OF REASON

On Monday morning Serena was the first person awake in her household. She rolled out of bed and checked on her sister Annie, who was asleep in her room. Serena moved the baby's crib into her room last night because their mother worked a late shift and wouldn't get off until three a.m. Serena thought Princess would retrieve her youngest child when she got home, but Annie was still sleeping soundly in the crib. Serena smiled as she reached down and gently touched her face.

She turned on the lights and told Sheila to wake up before she left the room to do the same for Paul. Paul was known to roll over and continue sleeping after his wakeup call, so Serena didn't leave his room until he was up and sitting on the side of the bed.

She went to the bathroom to wash up, and then she went to the kitchen to get breakfast started. She found enough instant oatmeal for everyone. She got a pot of milk boiling on the stove while she made a bottle for Annie. By the time she got back to her bedroom, the baby was awake and grumpy. Serena changed her diaper and fed her before taking Annie to her mom's bedroom.

Princess didn't wake up fully, but she mumbled something that sounded like, "Hey Serena."

"Hi, Mama."

Serena placed the baby next to her mom, and Princess reached for her instinctively without opening her eyes.

"You fed her?" she murmured.

"Yes. And changed her. I'll be back with her crib in a sec'."

Princess didn't respond to that.

Serena lugged Annie's crib back to her mother's room, and then she checked on Sheila and Paul. Both were up and nearly dressed. Serena went to turn the burner off on the stove before she quickly got dressed herself. When she was done, her brother and sister were both ready for breakfast. Serena prepared the oatmeal and gave them a granola bar and a cup of orange juice as well.

Fifteen minutes later the three of them left the building and were greeted by bright morning sunshine.

Serena hated all of her chores and "sisterly duties" most of the time. But sometimes, like this morning, everything fell perfectly into place, and she didn't mind at all. She loved her family, and when she took care of them, it made her heart feel warm and full.

Jamar was right; she would make a great mother one day.

● ● ● ● ● ●

Serena had to walk her sister to grade school and then walk her brother to middle school before she made the final

trek to Finley High. Paul was sometimes resentful of her
presence, but Serena rarely let him walk alone. He was at
that tender age where boys started to pick the path they
wanted to follow in their scholastic career. Some of his 7th
grade classmates were already skipping school and getting
high. Serena knew that a lot of her little brother's decisions
were out of her control, but the least she could do was make
sure she watched him enter the school every morning.

When she got to school herself, her day went well
until lunchtime. Serena's best friend Cicely showed up at her
locker during passing period and asked, "Are you going to
your bible club meeting today?"

"Yep. Every Monday and Friday."

Serena expected her friend to give her a hard time
about it, which she was no longer bothered by.

But Cicely surprised her by saying, "I wanna come
too."

Serena closed her locker and turned to stare at her,
wondering what kind of foolishness her buddy had in mind.

"What?" Cicely said. "I can't go to your bible club
meeting?"

Serena continued to knit her eyebrows. "Yeah, but
why? Why you want to go now?"

Cicely shrugged. "You've been going for so long, I
want to know what the big deal is."

"There's no big deal," Serena told her. "All we do is
talk about the bible. It's actually kinda boring."

"So you don't want me to go?"

Serena did not, in fact, want her friend to go to the
meeting. But she wasn't sure why. Even if she could put her
finger on it, she couldn't very well turn someone away from
learning about Jesus. She decided it was Jamar she was

worried about. Her friends were never nice to him. She didn't want to bring anyone to the meeting who would make him feel uncomfortable.

"What do you want to do, find something else about Jamar to make fun of?" she guessed.

"No. I'm not going to make fun of him, Serena. I told you; you've been going to those meetings, and I'm curious about it, that's all."

"You don't even go to church," Serena told her.

"I have to go to church before I can go to your bible meetings?" Cicely asked the question like she knew that was definitely not the case.

"I just don't want you starting any trouble."

"You sure are protective of Jamar..."

Now Serena was growing frustrated and anxious. Again, she didn't know why she was feeling either of those emotions. One of Jamar's major goals for the bible club was to attract new members. Could Serena turn a potential member away, just because she was worried about her motives?

"Alright, come on," she said. "I swear, if you do anything stupid..."

"Ain't nobody gonna mess with your boyfriend," Cicely assured her.

"He's not my boyfriend."

"Yeah, whatever," Cicely said and followed her friend down the bustling hallway.

● ● ● ● ● ●

The bible club meeting that afternoon was one of the best so far. Including Mrs. Harding, twelve people attended.

Jamar divided them into three groups and provided each group with a huge roll of aluminum foil. He instructed the teams to craft a sword, shield, helmet, belt and a breastplate from the foil and decorate one of their members in the outfit. When they were done, everyone voted on who had the best suit of armor, and then they read from the bible; *Ephesians 6, verses 10-18*, which referenced the armor of God.

Serena thought the visual representation was great, and she was proud of the way Jamar was leading the group. But she remained anxious throughout the meeting, because she still thought Cicely was up to something. Fortunately the meeting ended without incident.

Serena offered to help clean up before the bell rang, announcing the end of their lunch break. She was not happy when Cicely volunteered to straighten up the classroom as well. Serena had to dig deep inside her heart to find out what was really troubling her. While it was true that she didn't want Cicely to do anything mean to Jamar, there was something else that bothered her even more.

Serena couldn't deny the fact that she was jealous of sharing Jamar. That feeling made her feel icky and unsure of herself for the next hour.

● ● ● ● ● ●

After school Serena became guarded when her best friend approached her locker again.

"I had fun at the meeting today," Cicely reported. "I think I'm gonna start going every time."

Serena bristled, and she tried her best to hide it. "That's fine. The more the merrier."

"Are you okay?" her friend asked. "You been acting funny all day."

Serena sighed. She kept her eyes averted as she busied herself in her locker. "I told you; I didn't know why you wanted to come to the meeting. You were never interested in religion before."

"You weren't either," Cicely said. "Not until you got pregnant."

Serena turned to her, her eyes wide, her mouth open.

Cicely looked around and said, "Relax. Didn't nobody hear me."

"I still don't want to talk about that at school," Serena hissed.

She now wished she hadn't told Cicely about her dilemma, but at the time Serena felt terrified and alone. Her period was late, and her boyfriend Cedric had seemingly disappeared from the face of the Earth. It was Cicely who went with Serena to get a pregnancy test, and it was Cicely who comforted her when the results came back positive.

The whole ordeal brought them closer than they had ever been, but now Serena wished she had done it all by herself. Her secret could never be one hundred percent safe as long as there was one person out there who knew all of the ugly details.

"Have you told Jamar yet?" Cicely wanted to know.

Serena couldn't believe her friend wouldn't drop it.

"No. You know I haven't."

"Why not?"

"Because I don't want anyone to know. I already told you that."

"I know you don't want a bunch of people knowing about it. But Jamar's taking you to the prom. Don't you think he has a right to know?"

"A *right*? How you figure that? He's not my boyfriend."

"You act like he's your boyfriend."

"No, I do not."

"Well, he acts like you're his girlfriend."

Serena wished she could deny that as well, but she couldn't. When Jamar first asked her to go to the prom, she thought he made it clear they would only be going as friends. But ever since she accepted the invitation, it started to feel like she'd agreed to be his girlfriend. The only thing missing from their *friendship-turned-relationship* was the kissing and hugging.

That wouldn't have been a bad thing under normal circumstances. Jamar was smart and handsome. And he was certainly not the type of guy to get Serena in any kind of trouble. But their circumstances were anything but normal. Jamar was a hardcore Christian with a bright future ahead of him, while Serena was a pregnant, teenage sinner who hadn't spoken to the boy who knocked her up in months. There was no way she and Jamar could ever have a real relationship. It would be sheer folly for her to think anything different.

"We're not in a relationship," she insisted.

"But he's taking you to the prom," Cicely pressed. "Jamar's a nice guy. If you don't tell him, you're making a fool out of him."

"He's a nice guy? Really? I've been telling you that for weeks, but now you wanna agree with me?"

"I never said he wasn't nice, Serena."

"No, you just chose to make fun of him every chance you got."

"No, I didn't. That was Toya and Cassandra."

"It was you too!"

"Alright. I'm sorry. I didn't mean to. Okay?"

"You don't owe me an apology. You can apologize to him, if you want to."

"Fine. I will. Now are you going to tell him you're pregnant?"

Serena's whole body heated to an uncomfortable level. She had to fight hard to keep her hands off of her friend. She was itching to slap Cicely until the words coming out of her ugly mouth didn't hurt anymore. But violence wouldn't solve this problem. As a matter of fact, Cicely would probably blab Serena's business to everyone, if they got into a fight.

"Hey. How y'all doing?"

Serena turned and saw that the boy (who was not her boyfriend) had showed up to walk her out of school again. She was so stressed, she nearly told him to go away.

Before she could say anything, Cicely stepped past her and approached Jamar. Serena expected the worst, and her heart kicked hard in her chest.

"Hi," Jamar said. "Thanks for coming to the meeting today, Cicely. I'm really happy you decided to stop by."

Serena stared at him like he had the word SUCKER tattooed on his forehead. He had no idea what the girls were talking about before he approached. He was completely blind and ignorant, like a newborn gazelle stumbling past a horde of hyenas.

Serena wondered if she was in fact playing Jamar for a fool. Did he have a right to know about her condition? She quickly decided that he did not. Why would he? Everyone's medical information was their business. If she had sickle cell, was she required to tell him about that as well?

Jamar never even said he liked her, so as far as Serena was concerned, they were just friends – nothing more. He could show up at her locker *every* passing period, and it wouldn't change that.

"I wanted to apologize for anything I've ever done to offend you," Cicely said to Jamar. "You're a really nice guy, and you didn't deserve it."

Jamar was clearly confused by her change of heart, but he was also quick to forgive.

"Oh, that's fine. It's no problem. I can't think of anything you ever did to offend me."

"It's nice of you to say that," Cicely replied, "but you know it's not true. I know how me and my friends treated you, and I'm sorry."

"It's fine," Jamar insisted. "I forgave y'all a long time ago."

Cicely looked back at Serena with an expression that said, *Okay, now it's your turn,* before she walked away from them.

Serena sneered at her, but she fixed her face by the time she and Jamar made eye contact.

"That was unexpected," he said with a goofy, naïve smile.

"Very," Serena agreed. "That girl is full of surprises."

CHAPTER EIGHT
ROBYN

"Don't forget, you have to tell me where you live, so I can pick you up on Saturday," Jamar said as the unofficial couple exited the school together.

The date was May 4th, and the skies above Overbrook Meadows were powder blue. If Serena wasn't in such a sour mood, she might have taken a moment to admire the beauty Mother Nature provided them.

"I live in the projects," she said. When delivering bad news, it's best to get it over with as quickly as possible.

But Jamar didn't seem to care one way or the other.

"The Powell projects?"

"Yes," Serena said, her eyes narrowed. "You know about them?"

"I've never been. I've always heard they're dangerous."

She nodded. "Sometimes they are. You're not afraid to go there?"

"No. Not on prom night. I don't think there's anywhere I wouldn't go to pick you up this Saturday."

Serena wanted to comment on his obvious flirting, but she didn't know what to say. Instead she asked, "You're picking me up by yourself? You drive?"

"I do drive," he said proudly. "Got my driver's license and everything. The only reason I don't drive to school is 'cause I got into a wreck last year, and my dad took my car keys. He said he'll give them back when I graduate. I made his insurance go up a hundred and something dollars." He chuckled. "My bad."

"What kind of car do you have?"

He shook his head. "It doesn't matter."

"What does that mean? You don't wanna tell me?"

"People always act funny when I talk about stuff like that," Jamar revealed.

Now Serena was even more curious. "Why would they act funny? What is it, a Mercedes?"

"No. A Porsche."

Her eyes widened. "You have a *Porsche*?"

"Not a new one."

"Dang, Jamar. You really are rich."

"No I'm not. I told you: I don't have any money. It's my dad who has all the money."

"Why are you going to this school?" Serena wondered. "Shouldn't you be in a private school somewhere?"

"My dad didn't want to raise us like that. He said we'd be spoiled, if we grew up around a bunch of rich kids. He said we're no better than anyone else, and I agree with him."

Serena was completely blown away. It was a shame she waited until her senior year to get to know Jamar. He was such a mystery, wrapped in an enigma. Every layer she unraveled produced more questions, rather than answers.

"My mom's here," he said, his eyes locked on a vehicle in the parking lot.

Serena followed his gaze and saw a pearl white Mercedes idling with a Hispanic woman behind the wheel and Jamar's little sister Robyn sitting in the passenger seat.

"I knew you had a Mercedes," she joked.

"I don't have anything," he said. "My dad–"

"Yeah, Jamar. I get it."

"Hey, do you want a ride home?" he offered. "My mom can drop you off at your house."

"No," she said quickly. "I have to walk to Wedgewood Middle to pick up my little brother. And then we have to walk to Sunrise Elementary to get my little sister."

"Really? That's a lot of walking."

"All three schools are less than a mile apart," she told him. "It's not that far."

"We can pick up your brother and sister, too," Jamar said.

Serena checked out his ride again, and her heart froze. Now both of the Mercedes' passengers were staring at them. And the look she was getting from Jamar's little sister was downright acidic.

Robyn was younger than Jamar by one year. Serena never had any direct interactions with her, but she always thought the girl was pretty. Or maybe she felt that way because of a low self-esteem gene that was prevalent in a lot of black people. It clouded your vision and made biracial girls with straight hair appear to be more attractive than girls with pure, dark skin and kinky hair.

Whatever the case, Serena didn't think Robyn was pretty now. If looks could kill, Serena would've turned into a pile of dust because of the way Jamar's sister was glaring at her.

"No. I gotta go," she told Jamar and immediately began to walk away from him.

"Wait," he called. "My mom wants to meet you!"

"Not now," Serena said and continued marching in the opposite direction. She kept her head down and her eyes averted, but she could still feel the people in the fancy car watching her and judging her.

• • • • • •

"Mijo, why didn't you bring your friend over here so I can meet her?" Jamar's mother asked when he settled into the back seat. "Isn't that the girl you're taking to the prom?"

Olivia had dark, brown skin and a thick, Mexican accent. She was born south of the Texas border in Juárez, Mexico. Jamar's mom came from a long line of hardworking migrants. Even though she married an American, she remained proud of her heritage and was deeply rooted in her culture.

Jamar was happy to have a Mexican mother and a black father. He thought both of his parents had rich bloodlines and significant histories. But at the moment, he was too angry to appreciate anything, including his mother's accent.

"Robyn chased her away," he growled and pushed the back of her seat with his knee.

"You better quit," his sister warned without turning to face him.

"Hey, what's the matter?" their mother asked. She looked from Robyn to Jamar and saw they were both upset. "What happened?"

"Why were you looking at her like that?" Jamar barked at the back of his sister's head. "I saw you!"

"*What is going on?*" Olivia rarely saw her son this upset. "Why are you yelling? Tell me what happened. *Now!*"

"Jamar's dating a ho!" his little sister announced. She had her arms folded over her chest, her lips poked out in a serious pout.

Olivia's eyes and mouth flashed open at the same pace.

"*Robyn!* Watch your mouth! What is wrong with you?"

Jamar kicked the back of her seat again at the same moment. "Shut up! You don't know what you're talking about!"

"I do know what I'm talking about!" Robyn wailed. "That girl's a *ho*, Mama! Everybody knows it!"

Olivia hadn't spanked either of her children in years, but she instinctively winded up a vicious backhand before she caught herself. Her face was tomato red. Rather than strike her daughter, she grabbed Robyn's arm roughly and gave her a good shake.

"*You watch your mouth! Don't use words like that! You know I taught you better!*"

"Alright, she's a *whore*," Robyn spat defiantly.

"*Aye!*" Olivia released her and clasped her hands together to keep from lashing out again.

"You don't know anything!" Jamar yelled from the backseat. "You're evil! You're a liar!"

"*Stop it!*" their mother screamed. "*Both of you! Stop it!*"

Olivia was accustomed to outbursts of this nature from her daughter, because Robyn never fully accepted the Christian values everyone else in the family adhered to. She came to church with them every Wednesday and Sunday, but for her it seemed like a chore, whereas Jamar was always eager to get to the house of worship.

"If you don't like Jamar's friend, that's fine," Olivia told her daughter. "But don't call her names!"

"But Mama–"

"No, Robyn! *That's enough*! You can explain this to your father. *Both of you!*"

The teenagers were both seething with fury, but neither of them had anything to say after that. Their father Stephen was a kind, patient man. But he was also a strict disciplinarian who didn't tolerate disrespect from his children. Not one bit. He also didn't tolerate any disrespect towards his wife.

Robyn knew she'd already gotten herself in a good deal of trouble because of the way she spoke to her mom. She wisely decided to hold her tongue and her peace for the rest of the ride home, even though her brother's stupidity made her eyes burn with tears.

• • • • • •

When they got home, Robyn and Jamar retreated to their bedrooms without speaking. Olivia didn't bother trying to get to the bottom of their dispute without her husband there. In the past Robyn was usually proven to be in the wrong when she argued with her big brother. But Olivia knew that Robyn had more street smarts than Jamar.

If Robyn thought her brother's new friend was sexually promiscuous, she was probably correct. But Olivia also knew that Jamar wouldn't let some random hussy sway him from his Christian identity. At least she hoped he wouldn't. The sad fact was there were far too many temptations for boys and girls these days. If it wasn't sex, it was drugs. If not drugs, they still had gangs and peer pressure to contend with.

"Dios lo bendiga," she breathed as she put a pot roast in the oven and set the kitchen timer.

● ● ● ● ● ●

The Copeland family lived in a two-story home that featured five bedrooms, three and a half baths, a garage big enough for three vehicles and a big backyard with ten acres of beautiful green grass. The master of the estate pulled into the circular drive at six-thirty p.m. and snatched his briefcase from the passenger seat before exiting his vehicle.

Stephen Copeland was a large man, both tall and stout. His height teetered over six feet when he was a freshman in high school, and he still had three more inches to grow.

As impressive and imposing as he was physically, Stephen had always been a gentle giant, gravitating towards books and comics rather than athletic feats. He graduated with a degree in aeronautical engineering from Texas A & M and was still employed at Boeing, the first company to hire him fresh out of college.

Though he helped develop and build military aircraft for a living, most of which could be considered weapons of mass destruction, Stephen remained peaceful and godly throughout his adult life. He was a stern man who didn't like slackers or any worldly vices that went against his faith. He met Olivia at church two decades ago, and they were wed within four months.

As head of his household, Stephen governed with patience and kindness as well as strict discipline. Before he had a chance to take off his tie, his wife told him about the argument his children had after school. Stephen was very displeased, but he did not confront them right away. He waited until Olivia called them down for dinner. He watched his children eat in silence, both of them avoiding eye contact with everyone at the table.

When Olivia took their plates away, Stephen said, "Wait. Both of you remain seated," before his son or daughter could return to the relative safety of their bedrooms.

"Your mother tells me there was an argument," he stated. Stephen had a deep voice that sometimes felt like an eighteen-wheeler rumbling through their home. He looked slowly from Robyn to Jamar.

Their father wasn't an overtly handsome man, but his size, power and prestige added to his looks. He wore a thick moustache and a pair of wire-rim glasses that never made him look nerdy.

"Well, don't y'all both speak at the same time," he bellowed.

Robyn was generally obedient to her father, but she wouldn't repeat the things she said in the car earlier today, even if that meant defying him.

"Robyn said some bad things about Jamar's friend at school," their mother offered, which saved Jamar the trouble of snitching on his little sister.

Stephen's head slowly swiveled in Robyn's direction. The girl swallowed so hard, everyone saw the muscles in her throat flex.

"What did you say about Jamar's friend?" he asked.

"I told him she sleeps around," Robyn said quietly.

"Were those the words you used?" Stephen asked knowingly.

Robyn brought a hand to her mouth and began to nibble her fingernail. She hated the way her father asked questions he already knew the answer to.

She lowered her gaze and said, "I said she's a whore."

Stephen's nostril's flared. "I think you need to apologize."

Robyn looked up at him and sighed heavily as her eyes rolled in Jamar's direction. "I'm sorry," she mumbled. Before Jamar could respond, she added, "But she is."

Stephen shook his head in disappointment. His attention moved to Jamar. "Is this the girl you're taking to the prom?"

Jamar nodded.

"What's her name?"

"Serena," he said. "And she's not a whore."

"I don't want to hear that word again at this table," Stephen said with a grimace. He looked at Robyn. "But if you're going to make those kinds of accusations, I hope you have some kind of proof..."

His words hung in the air for several seconds, but she didn't respond.

"Well, do you?" he barked.

Robin flinched and sat up straight. "Everybody knows it," she said.

"I never heard anything like that," Jamar argued.

"That's because you don't hang around anybody who knows anything."

"And you only hang around *gossipers* who spread lies."

"It's not a lie."

Stephen interrupted their banter. "You still haven't given us proof of anything," he said to Robyn.

"She had a boyfriend named Marcus, and she slept with him," the girl said. "He took a picture of her naked, and he brought it to school and showed everybody. He got suspended for it. That was last year."

The revelation made all of the blood drain from Jamar's honey brown cheeks.

Stephen brought a large hand to his face and rubbed his forehead slowly. "You know this for a fact?"

"I have a friend who takes classes with her," Robyn said. "She knows her. I asked her about Serena, when she started going with Jamar."

"I'm not going with her," Jamar interjected, but it was clear that he had lost most of his poise.

"So you don't even know her," their father surmised. "Your opinions about this girl are based on hearsay."

"My friend doesn't have a reason to lie," Robyn told him. "Plus everybody knows why Marcus got suspended."

The big man at the head of the table fixed a chilling glare on his only begotten son. "You knew about this?"

Jamar's mouth was completely dry. He shrank under his father's gaze and looked down at his empty placemat. He shook his head.

"What other things are being said about this girl?" Stephen asked his daughter.

Robyn shook her head. Her eyes glistened with tears. "That's it."

Stephen turned back to his son and sighed loudly. Jamar felt the heat from his exhalation all the way across the table.

"What say you, boy?" His volume was only a notch above normal, but it felt like the whole house shuddered. "I take it you still want to go to the prom with this person."

It took every bit of strength Jamar had in him to lift his head and look his father in the eyes. He didn't fear that his father would physically harm him. But the weight of knowing that he had disappointed his dad was a terrible burden. He lived to please this man.

"Yes, sir. I, I can't cancel now. Prom is only a week away. If Serena did those things..."

He shuddered involuntarily. He didn't want to imagine pictures of Serena's nude body being captured and revealed on a cellphone. But he couldn't help it. Wicked, dirty images filled his mind – images he was revolted to think about at the dinner table.

"If she was that kind of person," he said, "then she has already changed. Or she wants to change. She might stop coming to the bible club, if I leave her hanging. She may turn away from the bible altogether. Wouldn't God want me to forgive her?"

"You're not God," Robyn informed him.

"Shut up!" Jamar shouted.

"Calm down," their father said. "Both of you!"

In the immediate silence that followed, Jamar threw in his last argument: "We're not going out, Dad. We're only going as friends. Nothing bad is gonna happen."

Stephen held a hand up in exasperation. When he had everyone's undivided attention, he said, "Son, understand this: If you weren't eighteen years old and about to graduate in a few weeks, I would absolutely *forbid* you from ever speaking to this girl again. She has lost her sexual purity, and I wouldn't want her anywhere near you. Understand that."

Jamar did understand. He found his dad's comment both frightening and liberating, because it sounded like that wasn't the final word.

"But you are eighteen," Stephen continued. "You'll be leaving for college this year. I have to trust that your faith is strong enough, at this point, for you to make the right decisions and maintain your own purity – even in the face of temptation..."

Jamar nodded quickly. "Of course, Dad. I'm not having sex until I get married."

In the background, he thought he heard his mom gasp slightly.

"I know your mother doesn't want to hear this," Stephen continued, "but you're a man, Jamar."

Olivia shuddered and wrapped her arms around her body. She stared at her dear son and smiled slightly. Jamar was surprised to see tears in her eyes.

"You have a soul filled with empathy," Stephen continued. "If God gave you this passion, I won't crush your spirit, Jamar. You can go to the prom with this girl, if that's your decision."

Everyone at the table reacted but slightly on the outside. On the inside their responses were monumental. Jamar had yet to recover when his father added, "But you must be respectful of your sister's feelings. If rumors start to spread about you, Robyn will be impacted. You get to leave Finley High for good at the end of the month. But Robyn has to return for another year..."

Jamar nodded. He didn't know what he could do to help that situation, but he did understand his sister's dilemma.

"And Robyn, you have to be respectful of your brother's feelings," Stephen said. "We got it all out on the table now. If Jamar chooses to continue to associate with this girl, it's his decision. This is his life, and you have to let him live it. I don't want you to do anything foolish, like lash out at that girl, either at school or when you see her at the prom."

It took a while, but Robyn nodded too. A fiery tear spilled from her eye. "Alright." Her voice was faint and not fully convincing.

Jamar wasn't sure if he believed her or not, but he appreciated the dialogue and he appreciated his father for always being level-headed and fair. He couldn't imagine what his family would be like without his father in the picture. He didn't think any child should have to experience that.

"Alright, well if that's it, I'd like to have some desert now," Stephen said. "How about you guys?"

Jamar and Robyn nodded their agreement, and their mother left her seat to retrieve a pie she baked.

"I'll be right back."

Jamar watched his father stare at his wife's backside as she walked away. It warmed his heart, to know that his parents were still physically attracted to each other after all these years. That was the kind of love he hoped to find when he was older.

● ● ● ● ● ●

An hour later Jamar lounged in his room with his cellphone in hand and his crush on the other end.

"It's okay," he told her. "Nothing has changed. We're still going to the prom."

"Did she say what she doesn't like about me?" Serena asked.

Jamar was hesitant to reveal his sister's grievances. If Serena didn't want to discuss her troubled past, he didn't want to tell her that he already knew. Sometimes honesty is *not* the best policy.

"She said you're not a virgin," he said reluctantly.

Serena wasn't surprised by that, but she asked, "How would she know?"

"She, um, she said she has a friend who knows you."

Serena's heart was in the pit of her stomach. She wondered who had been talking about her. She immediately thought about what happened with Marcus, because that horrible incident nearly caused her to transfer to a different school last year. The bullying got so bad. It was troubling to know that the story continued to linger around the hallways at Finley High. But whoever Robyn got her information from didn't know the worst of it, or Jamar would've asked if she was pregnant.

"I'm not a virgin," she confirmed.

"I don't care about that."

"I'm not a ho, either." She felt as lowly as she did when the Marcus scandal initially blew up at school. Back then she felt like she had to explain herself to *everyone*. Every time she thought it was over, someone else would find out about the picture, and she'd have to defend herself all over again.

"Serena, we don't have to talk about it. It's in your past, isn't it...?"

She swallowed hard. Marcus was in her past, and so was Cedric. But the end result of her bad deeds was still growing strong. Soon she wouldn't be able to hide it anymore. It would be big enough for everyone to see.

"Yes," she said.

"Okay. Then we can drop it. I don't want to upset you."

"I don't know why your sister is mad at me," she said. "It's not like me and you are going together. Did you tell her we're just friends?"

Jamar's heart thumped slow and hard. He knew they weren't in a relationship, but his feelings for Serena had evolved past mere friendship. It appeared that he was the only one who felt that way, like so many other times in his past.

"Yes, I told her that," he said. "She promised not to say anything to you at school or at the prom."

Serena thought he sounded disappointed now, but she wasn't sure why. "Okay. I'm not going to worry about it then, if you aren't."

"No. There's nothing to worry about," Jamar said. "We're gonna have a great time. You'll see."

CHAPTER NINE
MARCUS & LIL C

One day, a cold one
Late in December
The night of the party
I barely remember
I had sex, and although it was great
He lied about the condom
Wow, just great
I can't tell my mom
Someone help me!

But no one can ever know

    The rest of the week seemed to speed by. By the time Saturday rolled around, Serena was so antsy, she woke up at eight a.m. and couldn't convince her brain to go back to sleep for a couple more hours. She lay in her bed wide awake, staring up at the ceiling with a big smile on her face. Prom was only ten hours away. She couldn't wait to see what Jamar looked like in his tuxedo.

    She wondered if he would pick her up in his Porsche. She had never ridden in one before. She couldn't wait to put

on her dress and makeup. She and Jamar would look like
movies stars when they arrived at the venue. She wondered
if they would walk in arm in arm. He wasn't her boyfriend,
but proms were supposed to be romantic, weren't they? She
wouldn't mind if he held her hand, and she certainly wanted
to slow dance with him.

By ten o'clock she was out of bed and dressed in
shorts and a tee shirt. She made breakfast for her brother
and sisters and woke them up a few minutes later. They all
ate together in the living room while watching Saturday
morning cartoons.

Serena's mood was bright and infectious. Even the
stupid cartoons made her laugh. She practiced slow dancing
while she fed Annie her bottle. Paul and Sheila watched her
with envy. They begged her to bring them food from the
prom; a piece of cake, if possible. Serena didn't think there
would be any cake, but she lied and told them she would.

At noon her best friend Cicely called.

"Girl, what you doing?"

"Nothing," Serena said. "Trying to keep myself from
pacing around the house."

"I'm excited, too," Cicely said.

Unlike Serena, Cicely was actually in a relationship
with the boy who was taking her to the prom. Serena
expected their after-prom activities to be a lot more
interesting than whatever she and Jamar got into. Cicely
wasn't a virgin either, and she already purchased a three-
pack of condoms for this special night.

"Have you told Jamar yet?" she asked.

The question brought an immediate storm cloud over
Serena's sunny day.

"Told Jamar what?"

"You know what I'm talking about."

Serena's smile slipped away. She frowned and left the living room, in favor of the privacy of her bedroom.

"Why are you still talking about that?"

"Because I think it's *wrong*," Cicely said. "You know I love you girl. You're my best friend. But I can't sit back and watch you do somebody wrong like that."

"Since when are you so righteous?" Serena wondered. "You cheated on Byron two months ago."

"I know. But I told him," her friend said. "We talked about it, and he forgave me."

"He forgave you? That's probably because you didn't tell him *everything*."

"I did," Cicely insisted. "I even let him read me and Steve's text messages."

"Well, you *had* to tell him," Serena said. "You been going with him all year. He deserved to know."

"Jamar deserves to know, too."

"*But I'm not going with him*," Serena stressed. "Anyway, his sister already told him about me and Marcus, and he still wants to go to the prom with me."

"For real? What did she tell him?"

"She told him I'm not a virgin anymore – because apparently that's a big deal to them people..." She said it like Jamar's family were the ones who were weird.

"What'd he say?"

"He still wants to take me. Nothing's changed."

"But–"

"Listen," Serena said, growing frustrated. "He's picking me up in *five hours*. What's the point of telling him now? I already bought my dress, and he got his tux and paid for the tickets. If I tell him today, he's either going to back out at the last minute, or we'll go, and he'll be looking at me funny the whole night. Either way, everything will be all messed up.

"I promise I'll tell him after tonight. I'll tell him as soon as we get back to school on Monday. If he decides he doesn't want anything to do with me after that, so be it. At least it won't ruin the prom."

Cicely sighed. "Alright, Serena."

Serena sighed too, glad that her friend was finally willing to let her handle this her way. And why shouldn't she? It was Serena's body they were talking about. No one should be able to dictate what she did with it or who she told about it.

"Why'd you let that boy get you pregnant?" Cicely wondered, not for the first time.

"I don't know," Serena breathed. She sniffled, and her eyes slowly filled with tears.

● ● ● ● ● ●

Cedric Cooper, better known as *Lil C*, was not the kind of guy any woman with self-respect would consider good husband or upstanding father material. But that was just fine with Serena, because when she met him, she wasn't looking for a husband or a baby-daddy.

Technically they met during her freshman year at Finley High, but Serena didn't have any classes or interactions with him that year. Cedric was an obvious nogoodnik, with nappy hair, dirty shoes and faded battle scars on his arms and knuckles. It didn't take long before the upperclassmen zeroed-in and bullied him for his disheveled appearance and obviously poor parents. The bullying lasted for only a week before Cedric stabbed a classmate with his number 2 pencil and was sent to an alternative school for the rest of the year.

Cedric returned to Finley High the following year, but he was still a freshman, while Serena had advanced to the tenth grade. At the time, she had a crush on another wannabe thug named Benjamin, so she never gave Cedric a second glance.

Her junior year was much of the same. Cedric's attendance at school was spotty at best, and he served a few months in juvenile detention for possession of marijuana on campus. By then Cedric had grown six more inches and was delivering packages for one of the dope peddlers in his neighborhood. The income he received allowed him to purchase a few pairs of Jordan sneakers and a flashy gold chain. Serena did notice him that year, but she considered herself a good girl, and everyone told her Lil C was bad news. The worst of the worst.

Cedric decided to give school one last earnest attempt during Serena's senior year, but they didn't speak for the first time at Finley High. Instead Serena ran into him in her neighborhood one bitterly cold morning in late January. Princess sent her to the corner store to get diapers for Annie, and Serena cursed her mom the whole way there.

"Why she have another baby in the first place?" she muttered under her breath. "I knew I was the one who was gonna have to do everything for her. Why can't she keep her legs closed?"

When she entered the store, Serena took a moment to shake off the winter chill before she headed to the appropriate aisle. Before she got there, she spotted a familiar face. Cedric squatted in front of a display of long, white tee shirts that all of the gangsters and dope boys in the city had taken a liking to. He looked up and his eyes narrowed slightly when he saw Serena.

"Don't I know you from somewhere?"

She nodded and then shivered. Her hands were jammed into her coat pockets, but her fingertips were still numb. "You, you used to go to my school," she breathed through icy shudders.

Cedric stood slowly. By the time he reached his full height, Serena found that she had to look up at him to meet his eyes. He had dark chocolate skin, thick eyebrows and short, wavy hair. His face was clean-shaven. His lips nice and pink. He wore faded blue jeans that were a little too long but fit him snugly around the waist. He wore a blue tee shirt with a New York style bomber jacket draped over it. His Nike sneakers were pristine white with dark blue shoestrings.

Serena didn't know if he morphed recently or if he had always been this fine, but his good looks rendered her temporarily speechless.

"I still go to your school," he said.

His teeth were almost perfectly straight. He had an old scar under his left eye that was nearly an inch long. It looked like someone had stabbed him in the face. Serena wasn't sure why, but the scar added to his looks, rather than take away from them. Overall he reeked of **DANGER**, but she found that intriguing, rather than frightening.

"Barely," she said.

His head cocked slowly to the side. "Huh?"

"I said *barely*. You barely go to school."

He grinned, and Serena's heart skipped a beat. He looked like a wolf sizing up a sheep he wanted to drag away to his den.

"You trying to be funny?"

She shook her head. "No."

"You look good," he said. "Why you ain't never holler at me at school?"

Serena blushed. She couldn't stop a smile from creeping to her face. That morning she had her hair wrapped and a stocking cap pulled over it. Her winter coat wasn't all that flattering, so she suspected it was her tight jeans that garnished the compliment.

"You got a fatty," Cedric confirmed. "I seen it."

Serena's mouth fell open. She had no idea how she should respond to that. Boys flirted with her from time to time, but never had one come right out and complimented her booty. On one level she thought she should be offended by the comment. But on another level, she was proud of her figure – her butt included.

"Turn around," he said. "Lemme see."

Cedric had the nerve to reach for her arm and try to turn her himself, which Serena found both mortifying and exhilarating. She jerked her hand away from him.

"Boy, you better stop!"

He chuckled. "I'm just playing."

Serena's eyes registered annoyance, but she couldn't wipe the darn smile off her face.

"I'ma see it when you walk away anyway," Cedric told her.

Serena realized he was right about that, and she was confused by his whole approach. At school she thought he was just another dumb kid. But outside of school Cedric was something else entirely. His confidence and the way he was staring at her heated her whole body, to the point that her fingers weren't even cold anymore.

"I gotta go," she said, sensing that was the only rational move she could make at that point.

"A'ight. Go," Cedric said. He folded his arms over his chest and held his ground. "I'ma watch."

"Watch what?"

"Yo fatty."

Serena couldn't believe they were having this conversation. Is this what real men were like? They just come right out and tell you they want to look at your butt?

"You a freak," she decided.

He nodded slightly. "Yeah."

Serena's eyes widened. That was even worse than him talking about her butt! Who the heck admits that they're a freak?

Rather than turn and walk away, she backed up until she made it to the aisle that had the diapers. Cedric never took his eyes off her. She rolled her eyes at him before heading down the aisle.

The moment she couldn't see him anymore, she let out a pent up breath. Her mouth was completely dry. She licked her lips and was horrified to find them dry and chapped. They were probably ashy white, for all she knew.

Oh my God! she thought. *I'm walking around looking like a crackhead!*

But if that was the case, why was Cedric so attracted to her?

He doesn't care about your face, stupid. He said he likes your fatty.

Serena knew the voice in her head was probably right, but she still checked to make sure she didn't have any stray hairs sticking out of her stocking cap before she headed to the register with her little sister's diapers.

But when she got to the front of the store, Cedric was gone. Serena was disappointed by that, and she wasn't sure why. What in the world was wrong with her? Did she want some loser who barely passed the ninth grade to touch and stare at her against her will? She had a dozen reasons why Cedric was bad news and couldn't come up with one good thing to say about him, except he was:

Handsome
Sexy
Fine
Manly
Tough
Dangerous
And he likes my fatty!

You got issues, she told herself. *You should be glad he's gone.*

Serena decided that advice was sound. She tried to push Cedric out of her head as she paid for the diapers. When she exited the store, the winter chill slapped her in the face, causing her eyes to water. She heard the booming system from someone's car a moment before she managed to focus her watery eyes on a Chrysler 300 that was idling in the parking lot. The car didn't have any fancy rims, but the windows were tinted and there was no body damage.

The speakers were so loud, Serena recognized the song that was playing before the driver rolled down the window. It was *Voyage to Atlantis* by the Isley Brothers.

She was surprised – but not really surprised – when the window came down, and she saw Cedric behind the steering wheel.

"You need a ride?"

"I live right down the street," Serena said, but she found herself approaching the sweet automobile.

"It's too cold out here," he told her. "Get in. Let me give you a ride."

"Is this your car?"

"Yeah. Just bought it."

Serena had a feeling he was lying about that.

"You got a driver's license?"

He shook his head. "Nope. What I need that for?"

Oh, this is bad...

"You got a baby?" he asked, noticing her purchase.

"No!" she said indignantly. "These are for my sister. What I look like, having a baby in high school?"

Cedric nodded his approval. "Alright, well hurry up and get in. I promise not to do anything stupid."

"You just want me to get in so you can look at my butt when I get out," she guessed.

"No, I just don't wanna see you walking," he said earnestly. "And I wanna holler at you. Looking at your butt when you get out is only a bonus."

Up to that point of her life, Serena had made quite a few bad decisions. Getting in the car with Lil C proved to be worse than all of them combined.

● ● ● ● ● ●

Over the next three weeks Cedric and Serena were nearly inseparable. He lived in a project unit with his grandmother right down the street, so she was able to hook up with him on a daily basis. Cedric could be really sweet at times. On the days he did go to school, he gave Serena a ride as well as her little brother and sister.

But he had a mean side, too. Serena once watched him attack another man who supposedly owed him money. The beating wasn't excessive, and the graphic scene only served to further her infatuation.

By Valentines' Day she swore she was in love with him, and Cedric said he loved her too. And since February 14th was the most romantic day of the year, Serena felt it was totally appropriate for her to offer him a very special gift.

Cedric had his way with her (when it happened, she would've described it as *making love*, but now that she knew better, *had his way* was more appropriate) on his grandmother's couch when she went out to play bingo that Saturday night. For Serena, the sex act united them like no words or promises ever could. Afterwards, as they lay sweaty and satiated, she knew that Cedric would be her man until they were old and gray. There was nothing she wouldn't do for him.

What Cedric wanted was to try a different position the next time they were intimate. It happened a week later, on Saturday, February 21st. Cedric's grandmother left to play bingo again, and they had the apartment to themselves. His new position had Serena facing away from him.

Later, Cicely asked why she couldn't *feel* that he didn't have a condom on. Serena thought that was ludicrous. That was only her fifth sexual encounter. She didn't think five attempts made her an expert on the subject. How was she supposed to *feel* a thin layer of latex?

But more importantly, why would Cedric do that to her? Did he want her to get pregnant? He did it on purpose? Cicely said boys don't like to wear condoms because they don't get as much sensation. But that was bull crap! Why would Cedric burden her with a child, just so he could have ten minutes of *full sensation*? Did he even care about what he was doing? Did he ever care about her at all?

Unfortunately Serena was still waiting for answers to those questions. By the time she realized her period wasn't coming, Cedric was long gone. His cheap cellphone was a throwaway, and apparently he had done just that: Thrown it away. Serena made countless trips to his grandmother's unit in search of him, but his car was never there. Eventually she mustered the courage to knock on the door anyway.

The old woman told her, "Ced' don't live here."

"But, but he was here a couple of weeks ago," Serena cried. "He was staying here."

"That's all he do," the woman said, shaking her head. "He stay here. He stay there. He stay wherever he want. But he don't stay nowhere long enough to call it home. That boy got problems, baby. I'm sorry."

Serena spent the following month searching for Cedric in every hallway at school and every corner of the projects, but he was never there. She cried for him many a night. She felt like her heartache was exacerbated by the fact that she had so many unanswered questions. In the end, the most important question was why she trusted him in the first place. She thought she'd learned her lesson after Marcus.

Marcus was the only other person she had sex with. They did it exactly three times. He was currently a senior at

Finley High, but thankfully they didn't have any classes together. Serena saw him often, though; usually in the cafeteria at lunch time. Each time they locked eyes, her heart began to kick hard with anger and humiliation, the same as it did when he first betrayed her: She foolishly allowed Marcus to take a picture of her bare breasts with his cellphone, and he promptly showed the pic to all of his friends at school the following Monday.

Marcus got in tons of trouble for that. He almost got arrested for sharing what the police described as "child pornography." But he wasn't the only one who felt the heat. Serena had loved him more than she loved herself. She loved him so much, she gave him the most valuable asset she had; something she'd been holding onto for seventeen years. But Marcus didn't respect her or her virginity. To him, Serena was just another locker room story that would garnish him kudos from a bunch of idiots who were just as brain dead as he was.

After Marcus, Serena swore off boys completely. But it didn't last long. She fell in love with Cedric and once again spread her legs for someone who didn't appreciate her. Of course things turned out much worst that time. What Cedric did to her made him a monster. As for Serena, she was clearly a fool. There was no other explanation. And now her life was about to take a drastic turn for the worse.

When she learned of her pregnancy, Serena nearly drowned in a sea of tears, regret and self-loathing. Instead of giving up on life, she followed the same route many sinners had gone before: She reached out to God. Her mother didn't understand her sudden surrender to a higher power, and her aunt didn't understand, and Jamar was probably curious about it as well.

But it wasn't for them to understand.

Serena needed to be healed in a way that no human hands could. She needed to build a foundation for her unborn child to grow on. That foundation wouldn't have a husband, an income or even a home in a safe neighborhood. But it would have a Christian mother at the helm, and that was more than most of the unborn babies in the projects had to look forward to.

For now, that was all Serena had to offer her child.

CHAPTER TEN
MONKEY WRENCH

It's been a month now, and I feel so sick
Throwing up everywhere
All I can say is blech!
My mom is getting suspicious
But I say I have a cold

No one can ever know

Jamar called thirty minutes after Serena got off the phone with Cicely.

"Good afternoon."

"Hey," she told him. She left her spot on the couch and retreated to her room for privacy. Her brother and sisters looked on with obvious interest. To them, Serena's life seemed incredibly awesome.

"Whatcha doing?" Jamar asked.

"Nothing. Watching TV. Trying not to put on my dress four hours early and wear it around the house."

He laughed. "Me too! I keep thinking my tux won't fit anymore, and it will be too late to get another one by the time I find out."

Serena liked that he was as excited and anxious as she was. "Why wouldn't it fit anymore?"

"I don't know. I'm sure it will. But I didn't try it on again when we picked it up. What if they put the wrong one in the bag for me?"

"Ooh, that would be bad. I took my dress to the register myself, so I know it still fits."

"Will you still go with me, if I have to wear regular church clothes?" he joked.

"Of course I will," Serena said, and then her heart fluttered, and she caught herself.

Her *feelings* were constantly getting in the way of their friendship. She supposed that would make prom night more special for them, more *romantic*, even. But there would be no romance between her and Jamar. And given her track record, that was not only for the best, but it was the only appropriate thing for them.

"So, are you driving your Porsche?" she asked as a distraction.

"No," he said.

Serena waited, but he didn't offer anything further. "Your dad still won't let you drive?" she asked.

"He probably would've, but I asked him if he could take us."

Serena's eyes widened. She didn't expect that at all.

"Your dad's taking us to the prom?"

"Is that alright?"

"Um, I guess so..."

"You sound disappointed."

"It's just, I don't know if I'm ready to meet your dad. If your sister doesn't like me, I'm sure she said some things to make your parents not like me either."

109

Jamar started to laugh, which was definitely not the response Serena anticipated.

"I'm just kidding," he said. "Sorry if I got you worried."

"You were kidding about what?"

"My dad's not taking us to the prom. He said I could drive."

"Oh." Serena was surprised by the huge wave of relief that washed over her. To her recollection, she'd never been ashamed to meet someone's parents before.

"Hold on," Jamar said. He came back to the line a moment later. "I gotta go. My dad wants me to do something for him."

"Okay." Serena thought about how nice it must be for a kid to have a father in his life. Jamar was probably the most well-rounded boy she knew.

"Don't forget, I'll be there at six o'clock."

"You know I'm not gonna forget."

"Alright. I can't wait."

"Me neither. Bye."

● ● ● ● ● ●

Serena's mother hadn't done anything thus far to help with the prom, but Serena certainly didn't think Princess wanted to derail her plans. That all changed at three p.m., when Princess finally made it home from whatever activities she was engaged in on Friday night. The last thing she told Serena when she left yesterday evening was, "I'm going out with Cheryl and them. Mama be back."

"Hey," Serena said when Princess stormed through the front door.

110

"Hey, y'all," Princess said. She was still dressed in the skirt and heels she wore last night, but her outfit wasn't wrinkled enough to suggest that she actually slept in it.

Serena was curious about what her mother had been up to since she left yesterday, but it was only a vague curiosity. Knowing the man's name wouldn't help any, and thinking about her mother sleeping around *again* would only serve to deepen her resentment.

Princess approached the couch and hefted her youngest daughter, who started reaching for her the moment she walked in.

"Hey, sugar baby."

Sheila and Paul were also happy to have their mother home. They immediately began to bombard her with questions about dinner and what plans she had for them while Serena was at the prom.

"Whoa, slow down," Princess said. "I just came home to get dressed for work. I have to leave in an hour."

Serena's mouth fell open, but her mother was still on the move. Princess toted Annie to the bedroom, with her oldest daughter quick on her heels.

"What do you mean you have to go to work?" Serena asked.

Her mother's bedroom was surprisingly neat, considering the impulsive nature of her lifestyle. Serena guessed that was probably because Princess didn't allow anyone to enter her room while she was away. And when she was there, she only had to share her space with the baby.

"I gotta go to work," Princess repeated. She stepped into her closet without looking back. "Janice is picking me up in an hour."

Serena still had a look of shock pasted on her face. She followed her to the closet and stood in the doorway.

"Mama, I have to go to the prom tonight! You can't leave!"

"Girl, what you mean I can't leave? I gotta go to work." Princess looked around the closet with annoyance. "Get out my light."

The closet was small, and the one light bulb overhead had burned out weeks ago. Rather than replace it, Princess was waiting on someone from the city to do it. She already put in a work order.

"If you pay rent, you don't have to fix stuff," she had told Serena on multiple occasions. "They gotta unclog your toilets, fix the garbage disposal and give us new batteries for the smoke detectors. *It's the law.*"

Serena was fuming, but she took a step to the side, so that the light from the bathroom could help illuminate the closet.

"Mama, you know I have to go to the prom tonight! What am I supposed to do about the kids?"

Serena's words registered the moment they left her lips, and her look of disgust intensified. Why in the world was she so concerned about what happened to Sheila, Paul and Annie? They weren't her kids!

"What are *you* gonna do about them?" she corrected herself.

"The prom ain't as important as me going to work," Princess said matter-of-factly. "Call your auntie or something. If you gotta go, you can find somebody else to watch them."

Serena thought the conversation was getting more absurd by the second. "Why do *I* have to find somebody, Mama? Those are *your* kids!"

Princess found the khaki pants and golf shirt she was required to wear to work, and she brought them out of the closet. She deposited the clothes on her bed and then did the same with Annie.

"You know we all have to help out in this house," Princess simply said.

She sat on the corner of the bed and rushed to take her heels off. She stood and removed her dress with the same haste. Serena thought her mother could use a membership card at *any* gym, but she also knew that her mother's voluptuous hips and thighs and mega breasts continued to attract men wherever she went. Apparently none of those men were good enough to be a *husband*, but quite a few of them were good enough to scratch Princess' temporary itch.

"Mama, I help out more than you do," Serena cried. Her eyes welled with tears as all of her magnificent plans came crashing down around her. "What if I can't find anyone to watch them?"

"You can't leave them here by theyself," Princess said as she headed for the bathroom. "You know that."

Serena did know that because her 14th birthday was a big deal in their household. Serena didn't know if it was the same in other states, but in Texas the legal age requirement to leave young children with another child is 14. In the years leading up to her 14th birthday, Princess would say things like, "*Girl, I can't wait till you turn fourteen, so I don't have to worry about y'all as much,*" or "*When you turn fourteen, I can finally get back to kicking it with my friends.*"

Serena didn't know what that meant at first, and she foolishly began to look forward to her fourteenth birthday. On that day, she would be considered a *big girl*. Serena later realized that her *big girl* title was synonymous for "full-time, live-in babysitter/maid," and she'd been duped by her loving mother.

Princess closed the bathroom door, thus ending their conversation. A second later, Serena heard the shower water come on. The tears were streaming down her face when she turned and saw Annie sitting in the middle of her mother's bed.

Serena hefted her sister and left the room with her. Annie hadn't seen her mother since she left last night at nine. It appeared that the eighty seconds they spent in the closet just now was the full extent of Annie's time with mama for today. With that in mind, Serena was able to keep a lid on her frustration, which was threatening to erupt like a volcano.

Serena's last day of high school was coming in a few weeks. She planned to get a job and move away from home as soon as her finances allowed. Annie, on the other hand, was barely at the beginning of her eighteen years of hell with Princess. Compared to her, Serena had a lot to be grateful for.

● ● ● ● ● ●

"I'm sorry, Serena. I can't do it tonight," Aunt Mary said. "Jimmie and I are going out for our anniversary."

The rejection caused Serena's waterworks to start anew, but she tried not to take it out on her aunt. Mary had been married to a great man for over twenty years. Despite the fact that she was tumbling down a pit of despair, Serena was happy for her.

"Okay, Auntie. Bye."

"Wait," Mary said before she could hang up. "Serena, are you alright?"

"Yuh, yes."

"Baby, stop crying. You, hold on a sec'."

Serena continued to rock the baby and run through a very small list of alternate baby-sitters until her aunt came back to the line. Her grandmother lived on the north side of town. She was an ill-tempered woman, but she would do it – but only if Princess took all three of the kids to her. Princess didn't have a car, so Serena didn't see how that was possible.

Maybe she could ask Jamar to drop her siblings off when he got there. Porches don't have backseats, but Serena was willing to strap everyone to the hood of his car, like an old mattress.

"What time are you leaving?" Aunt Mary asked when she got back to the line.

"He said he'll be here at six o'clock."

"Alright," Mary said with a sigh. "I'll be there."

Serena's heart was suddenly excited again, but she worried that the cost was too high.

"Wait. I thought it was your anniversary."

"I see Jimmie every day. We can go out any time. And our actual anniversary was Wednesday. Today's just the day we chose to celebrate."

"But, but I don't want you to miss out because of me."

"I'm not missing out on anything," Mary assured her. "I'm just going to wait until next weekend. It's no big deal."

"Yes it is."

"So you're saying you *don't* want me to come and babysit so you can go to the prom?"

"I do, but I don't... I don't know what I want."

"You want someone to help you, so you should let me do that. This is a very important day for you. We did *way* too much planning to let it go to waste because Princess doesn't have a babysitter. Where is she anyway? Why didn't she call me?"

"She's in the shower, getting ready for work. Do you want me to tell her to call you?"

"No," Mary said with undisguised disappointment. "I'm just glad she's had this job for so long. I certainly don't want her to get fired again..."

● ● ● ● ● ●

At four o'clock Serena got in the tub herself. She was so antsy, it took nearly forty-five minutes to do her hair and make-up when she got out. Her mom didn't have the money to send her to a salon yesterday, but Serena went to Cicely's house after school, and her friend styled her hair perfectly. She wrapped it up tightly before bed and was happy to see that her 'do was still intact. It just needed to be tweaked and puffed here and there.

For prom night, Serena wore her hair down, with reddish brown highlights that added contrast and depth. On the left side of her scalp, she had a dozen skinny cornrows that created a unique pattern before uniting with the rest of her mane. She kept her makeup soft and "barely there," but that didn't take away from her sister's look of awe. Sheila stood next to her at the bathroom sink and watched closely as she transformed from Serena the hood chick to Serena the seldom seen beauty queen.

Serena got caught up in the glamour herself when she put her dress and shoes on and admired her reflection in the mirror. As silly as it was, she really did feel like Cinderella. Her daily duties included cooking, cleaning, going to school, changing the baby, taking out the trash and other mundane tasks. But tonight she was dressed in her finest. She didn't even feel like her old self. This would be the best night of her life. She knew that before she stepped out of her bedroom at 5:45 and saw the look of wonder on her aunt's face.

"Oh my goodness, Serena! You are absolutely gorgeous!"

Aunt Mary left her seat on the sofa and stepped closer to admire her niece. She touched Serena's hair and dress and then hurried back to the couch to get her cellphone from her purse.

"Ooh, girl, you know I need some pictures!" Mary said as she took Serena's hand and pulled her to the other side of the TV where the lighting was better.

"You look amazing," she said as she snapped pic after pic. "Your mama's gonna hate that she wasn't here to see this!"

Serena doubted if that was the case, but she didn't allow any bad thoughts about Princess to spoil the moment. She posed for a dozen photos for her aunt with a radiant smile that was one hundred percent pure. Towards the end, her brother and sisters wanted in on the action, so Serena posed with them as well.

When someone knocked on the door at six p.m. sharp, Serena's heart came to a standstill. She stood stiffly in the living room while Sheila went to answer it. The little girl swung the door open wide and then stepped aside when she saw who it was.

"Come in."

Jamar smiled at Serena's little sister, and then his eyes bugged when he saw his date. He was so stunned, he didn't move at all until Sheila rudely repeated her statement.

"I said you can come in!"

"Sheila!" Aunt Mary admonished her. "Girl, go sit your tail down somewhere."

Sheila hopped on the couch grinning like a she-devil.

"Sorry about that," Aunt Mary said as she approached the door. "Please, come in," she told him.

Jamar walked into the apartment, his eyes still glued to Serena.

"You certainly are handsome," Aunt Mary told him.

Serena agreed with that one hundred percent. Jamar was always good-looking, but he really shined with formal attire. His suit fit him perfectly, and the tux added a few years to his age. Even though they were only going as friends, Serena knew she'd have the most handsome date at the prom. She couldn't think of one single boy at her school who took her breath away like Jamar did at that moment.

"Wow. You look really pretty," he said as he stepped to Serena. "I don't know what I expected, but I didn't expect this."

Serena blushed, and she had to look away. Her eyes fell upon two clear containers her date was carrying.

"Oh, these are for you," he said, but he only offered her one. "I mean this one is for you. The other one is for me."

"Ooh! Wait, wait!" Aunt Mary implored. She hurried to the couple and got her phone ready for more pictures.

"Okay. Go ahead!" She was all smiles. Serena was too, though she didn't know what they were supposed to do.

"Go ahead what?" she asked.

"You're supposed to put that corsage on his jacket, and you wear yours on your wrist," Mary instructed.

Serena looked into Jamar's eyes again, and she smiled weakly. She couldn't believe she was so nervous! Six weeks ago Jamar was a bible-thumping teacher's pet who wouldn't get a second glance from her. Now he was something different. Something more. Serena couldn't say exactly how much more, but she had a good feeling that whatever it was, the feeling was mutual.

"Thank you," she told Jamar as she cracked open her plastic case and admired her corsage.

She didn't know what type of flower it was, but it was beautiful and fresh. She brought it to her face and closed her eyes as she inhaled the sweet scent. She looked up at Jamar when she slipped the corsage on her wrist. She was surprised to see sweat on his forehead. He looked downright petrified.

"Are you alright?"

He flinched when she reached to wipe the beads of sweat off his face. Serena thought that was the first time she had ever touched him.

"Aww, y'all just too cute!" Aunt Mary said.

Serena gave her empty container to Paul, and she took the other one from Jamar. When she got it open, she asked her aunt, "Where do I put it?"

"On his lapel," she said. She stepped forward and pointed to the appropriate spot. "Right there."

Jamar tensed up even more as Serena affixed the corsage to his tuxedo. She thought his reaction was the cutest thing *ever*. Aunt Mary continued to take pictures, and then she positioned the couple in a few more poses so she could get even more shots.

Serena noticed that Jamar didn't really *hold* her when he put his arm around her, but that was fine. She knew that his interactions with the opposite sex had been limited, and she actually envied him for that.

"Alright, goodbye, y'all," Serena said when Aunt Mary finally had enough pictures and they headed to the door.

"Bye!" everyone responded. Even Annie waved goodbye to her sister.

"What time did your mom say you had to be in?" Aunt Mary asked.

Serena realized Princess hadn't given her a curfew for the night. She was suddenly embarrassed by her mom's lack of parenting.

"By one," she lied. She was sure most of her friends had later curfews than that, but Jamar's parents didn't seem like the type of folks who'd want their son out in the wee hours of the morning.

"Alright," Mary said. "Y'all be good!"

"We will!" Serena said, and then she opened the front door and was shocked to see a beautiful, black limousine parked on the curb. She looked back at Jamar, her eyes wide and disbelieving.

"Is that yours?"

He grinned. "Tonight it's *ours*."

Serena brought a hand to her face to cover her mouth, which was hanging open wide enough to shove an apple in it.

"What's wrong?" Aunt Mary said. Her smile was big and motherly.

"He, he got a limo," Serena managed.

"Ooh! I wanna see!"

Sheila rushed to the door, and the couple stepped aside to make way for her and Paul and eventually Aunt Mary and Annie as well. In all her years living in the projects, Serena had never once seen a limousine in her neighborhood.

She truly felt like a princess when she stepped out of her apartment and saw that a lot of her neighbors had come outside to check out the luxurious ride. The chauffeur left his spot behind the wheel, so he could hold the back door open for the young couple.

CHAPTER ELEVEN
PROM NIGHT

"Why didn't you tell me you were renting a limo?!"

Jamar grinned sheepishly. "I don't know. It was a surprise."

The beautiful couple lounged in the extravagant vehicle on a huge leather sofa that stretched nearly the full length of the limo and curved in the back. The couch was big enough to seat six adults, but it was just the two of them. Across from the sofa was an elegant bar that was stocked with wine glasses and beer mugs and a few bottles of champagne that were chilling in buckets of ice.

Overhead the roof looked like the ceiling of a night club, complete with neon lights and strobe lights and of course a huge sunroof that offered a sublime view of the auburn sunset and the first few stars twinkling in the night sky.

"Is it just us?" Serena asked. "Are we picking up someone else?"

She was too anxious to sit back on the sofa. Her smile was ear to ear. She sat on the edge of her seat and struggled to take it all in. Not only had she never been in a limo, but outside of funerals, none of her friends had either.

Jamar sat next to her looking a bit calmer as he admired her radiance, the way her smile glowed just as brightly as the lights that traced the bar.

"No, it's just me and you," he said.

Serena looked over at him and giggled. She knew she had to get her excitement under control, but that didn't seem like something she'd accomplish any time soon.

"What about your sister?" she asked. "Isn't she going, too?"

"Her boyfriend's taking her," Jamar said. "I don't know if he got a limo or not. I left before he got there."

"It's just so much space," Serena gushed. "We could've got three more couples in here."

"I thought about it," her date said. "But I didn't want you to be surprised to see them. I would've asked you ahead of time, but, like I said, I wanted the limo to be a surprise."

"Jamar, this is the best thing anyone's ever done for me!"

Serena had tears in her eyes as she threw both of her arms around him and hugged him tightly. She felt him stiffen in her grip, but she didn't let up. She knew he would loosen up at some point, as the night progressed.

When she backed away, she kissed him briefly on the corner of the mouth. But she regretted it immediately.

"I'm sorry. I didn't mean to."

Jamar appeared to be in a state of shock, with his mouth half open, his eyes big and beautiful.

"Oh, it's, that's alright," he said.

"No it's not," Serena replied. "You look like you've never been kissed before."

"Yeah I have–"

"That wasn't a real kiss anyway."

"That's fine, I–"

"Wait, did you say you *have* been kissed before?"

He frowned. "Serena, you know I'm eighteen years old, right?"

She laughed.

"My mom kisses me all the time," he said.

That cracked her up even more.

Jamar smiled, which she hoped indicated he was only kidding.

"So, you've had a girlfriend before?" she asked when her chuckles died down.

He nodded. "Yes, but I only kissed one of them."

Wow, Serena thought. *Eighteen years old, and he only kissed one girl*. Normally that would've made him the target of ridicule. It still would in most circles. But at that moment, Serena was in awe of him. She wished she could say the same about her past relationships.

"Did you love her?" she asked.

"Who?"

"The girl you kissed."

He frowned again, and Serena said, "I'm sorry. I don't mean to get all in your business. We never talk about this kind of stuff."

Jamar agreed that was true, and it was also a source of uncertainty as of late. Not only did they never talk about their past relationships, but they didn't talk about their current *situation* either. Jamar had no idea what to expect from Serena.

"I thought I loved her," he said. "But I was young. Only a sophomore."

124

"A *sophomore?* Jamar, that's probably old enough to know if you're in love."

He nodded but said, "My dad didn't think so."

"What happened to her?" Serena wondered. "Did he make y'all break up?"

He shook his head. "My dad wouldn't make me do something like that. I broke up with her on my own."

"Why, she wasn't a good kisser?" Serena joked.

"No. She cheated on me," he said matter-of-factly.

Serena's smile slipped away. "Oh. I'm sorry about that."

"It's fine," he said. "Water under the bridge. Every girlfriend I've had since the eighth grade either breaks up with me or cheats on me. And it's always for the same reason."

Serena felt like she was getting more than she bargained for with this conversation, but Jamar didn't look upset, so she asked the obvious question.

"What reason?"

He grinned. "Because I won't have sex with them."

Serena's face burned with embarrassment. She looked down at her hands in her lap. "Oh."

"Tell me something," Jamar said. He waited until they regained eye contact before he asked, "If we were going together, would you do that, too?"

Serena's eyes widened. This wasn't the Jamar she knew *at all.* This new Jamar was bold and confident in his beliefs. She never thought she'd see the day when *bible boy* intimidated her, but here they were.

"But we're not together," she said, purposefully avoiding the question.

"We could be," Jamar said quickly.

He didn't look nervous, and now Serena was nearly sweating bullets.

She shook her head. "No, we can't."

Jamar didn't look surprised by that response, but he asked, "Why not?"

"Because you don't know enough about me."

"Tell me what you think I need to know. Have you done something bad enough to run me off?"

Serena nodded slowly. Her eyes burned with tears. She didn't want to cry. It would ruin her makeup.

"Tell me," he urged her.

Serena's secret weighed on her so heavily, she felt her baby kick. She knew that wasn't physically possible. At the most she was only three and a half months pregnant. But she would've sworn she felt it.

She reached and took hold of his hand. She forced a smile.

"Can we please get through tonight? After the prom, I'll tell you anything you want to know about me. If you still want to go with me after that, I would be happy to be your girlfriend. But I don't think you will, and I will understand. *And*, to answer your other question, if we were going together, I wouldn't cheat on you or break up with you because you don't want to have sex."

Jamar stared at her for a few seconds while he processed that information. On one hand he was thrilled with the prospect of being in a relationship with Serena. It was rare that a crush he had on a girl was reciprocated. But on the other hand he knew that her secret must be really bad, if she thought it would make him run away from her. Was it the pictures that got her boyfriend in trouble last year? That was a big deal, but Jamar thought he could look past that, if she really had changed.

Prom would only last a few hours. He decided that he didn't want any dark clouds hovering over them tonight any more than she did.

"Okay," he said. "You can tell me after the prom."

"Great," Serena said, happy to avoid the inevitable for a little while longer. "So, what's up with this champagne?" she asked as she stood and approached the bar. "I know they didn't give you alcohol..."

"Limo companies don't give you anything." He stood as well. "Everything you want costs extra. And no, that's not champagne. It's sparkling grape juice."

Serena laughed. "I thought so!"

"Do you want some?" Jamar hefted one of the bottles.

"Yes. I want to experience everything this limo has to offer – especially *this*." She reached and touched the humongous sunroof.

"Do you want me to open it?"

"Yes. I want to stand on the sofa and hang out of it, like in the movies!"

"You can do that," Jamar said with a grin.

"I think I'll wait until we leave the prom," Serena said. "I don't want to mess up my hair."

"It looks beautiful," Jamar said, admiring the style.

"Why thank you," Serena said, and she selected a beautiful wine glass from the bar. "Fill 'er up, captain."

"Yes, ma'am," Jamar said as he removed the foil from the top of the bottle.

• • • • • •

Finley High School's prom was held in the ballroom of the downtown Hilton. Serena and Jamar felt like royalty from the moment they pulled up to the main entrance and waited for the driver to open the door for them.

Once inside, they encountered hordes of students who were all familiar, but some were nearly unrecognizable in their formal attire. Serena was surprised when Jamar reached to hold her hand, but she wasn't against the move at all. He made her feel safe and wanted. Serena still thought he was the best looking guy at her school – especially the way he looked tonight. She got confirmation of this from the first person to approach them. It was a girl she didn't know very well who usually hung out with the honor students' crowd.

"Oh my God, Jamar! Is that you?"

She stepped closer to get a better look. She was an Asian girl, petite and pretty. Her dress was fuchsia, and it was fashionable, but not as eye-catching as Serena's.

"You don't even look like yourself!" she exclaimed. Her eyes were wide. Her smile was as well.

"Hey, Kim," Jamar said. He left Serena's side to give her a hug. "You look great yourself! That dress is beautiful."

"Thank you! Have you seen Jessica? She's not gonna believe this!"

"No, I just got here," he said.

They stood admiring each other for so long, Serena felt a tad bit of jealously creeping up on her. Without knowing much about her, it looked like Kim would be a better fit for Jamar. Or maybe Kim was the girl who kissed him and then broke his heart. Serena kicked herself for not getting the name of that floozy.

"Have you met my date, Serena?" Jamar asked, turning her way.

"No, I don't think so," Kim said, seeming to notice her for the first time. "Wait. I've seen you around school – just never talked to you before," she told Serena. She looked her up and down. "Your dress is awesome!"

"Thank you! Yours is too," Serena replied.

"Come on. Let me take a picture," Kim said as she reached into her purse. She pulled out her cellphone and told the couple, "Okay, y'all. Get close!"

Jamar jumped at that opportunity. He put his arm around Serena and pulled her to him until there was no space between their hips. Serena was surprised by his newfound well of courage. She was grinning so much tonight, she thought her smile would look cheesy after a while. But her happiness was as real as the tremor that skipped down her spine each time Jamar touched her.

They encountered a lot more friendly faces before they made it to the ballroom. Some were friends of Jamar, others were Serena's friends. She hadn't noticed before tonight, but they had virtually no friends in common outside of the bible club. All of Jamar's classmates were blown away by the way he looked in his tux. They were equally amazed by the beautiful creature on his arm.

One of his buddies named Patrick Shinn pulled him aside and said, "How in the world did you get a babe like that to come to the prom with you?"

"I just asked her," Jamar said, his chest swelling with pride. "And she said yes."

"I asked a bunch of girls," Patrick complained. "They all said no, except her." He shot a thumb behind them, and Jamar saw that he came with Jameka Preston.

"She looks nice," he said.

"Yeah. All three hundred pounds of her!"

While Jamar was occupied, Serena looked around the lobby and squealed when she saw a group of her girlfriends hanging out near the entrance of the ballroom. She rushed to them, and they all hugged and admired each other's outfits.

"Girl, your dress is on *fleek*!" Cicely announced. "It's the best one here. I haven't seen anyone else wearing one like that."

"Thanks," Serena said. "Your dress is the bomb, too."

"Old ugly Felicia got my dress on," Toya snarled.

"She ain't the only one," Cassandra said. "Patrice's dress looks like yours, too."

"Where'd you get your dress from?" Toya asked.

"Dillard's," Serena replied.

"*Dillard's*? I went to J.C. Penney. Where'd you get *Dillard's* money?"

Serena couldn't help but feel flattered by all of the attention. "My dad sent it to me."

Toya was confused by that, because she knew Serena's father was locked up.

"I'll explain later," she told her.

"Bump all that," Cassandra said. "What I want to know is how you got Jamar looking so good tonight. Did you take him on that show *Extreme Makeover*?"

Her friends laughed at that, Serena included.

"No. I didn't do anything," she said. She spotted Jamar across the room, and all four girls began to stare at him. "Jamar always looks good. He just doesn't dress that good."

"Too dang preppy," Toya agreed. "But *umph*. He looking good tonight."

"Why you come with him?" Cassandra wanted to know. "You know he ain't gon' give you none when y'all leave."

"Believe it or not," Serena said, "there's a lot more to life than sex."

"*Nuh-uhn!*"

"It's true," Serena said sarcastically. "I know, it's shocking."

"So do y'all like, really like each other?" Cassandra wondered. "Or did y'all just come as friends?"

"We're friends. I do like Jamar. I think he likes me, too. But I don't think it would work, if we tried to have a relationship."

"Look at you," Toya said. "You done changed-up on us."

Serena continued to smile, and she didn't respond to that.

"What kinda car he got?" Cicely asked.

Serena's eyes lit up. "Girl, he picked me up in a *limo!*"

"Quit lying!"

"For real! Come on, it might still be out there!"

Serena led the way to the foyer with her friends trailing closely behind.

● ● ● ● ● ●

Once they finally made it inside the ballroom, Serena and Jamar were greeted by more photographers. This time they were professional. Their equipment was set up to use an elegant spiral staircase as the backdrop for the prom photos. After they snapped their pics, Jamar went to a nearby table to fill out paperwork that included payment information for the photos.

Serena told him, "You got to give me one of those prints! I want to remember what I looked like on the happiest day of my life!"

The Hilton ballroom was as lavish as Serena expected. The lighting was low, and there were strobe lights on the ceiling, along with a multitude of blue and white streamers than hung down, proudly displaying Finley High School's colors. There was a DJ booth in one corner and a huge dance floor right in front of it.

On the other side of the room, Serena saw two dozen round tables that were elegantly prepared. Each table had six chairs around it. Between the silverware (they had so many forks and spoons laid out, Serena knew she'd grab the wrong one) was a folded placard with a student's name on it.

Jamar and Serena found their spot, but it wasn't time to eat yet, so they didn't stay there. Instead they mingled with their peers, who were all dressed to the nines – with the exception of a few knuckleheads who wore sneakers with their tuxes. And of course there was the class clown, who didn't wear a tuxedo at all. Under his sports coat he wore a tee shirt with a tuxedo design on it. But everyone was having a good time, and no one complained, not even his date who was dressed to kill.

Over the next three hours Serena found the prom to be everything she expected it to be and a whole lot more. A lot of her teachers were there, and they were awfully proud of these young adults who had grown up right before their eyes.

"I remember when you were a freshman," Mrs. Diaz said as she pulled Serena in for a hug so tight it was almost uncomfortable. "Look at you now," she said when they separated. "You're a grown woman. And you're so beautiful!"

Serena was surprised to see tears in the woman's eyes.

For dinner they had honey chipotle glazed flank steak or eggplant parmesan for vegetarian diners. Serena still didn't know which utensils to use for each course of the meal.

She was grateful when Jamar leaned over and told her, "I don't know which one to use either. I just wait for Ana to pick one, and I do what she does."

On Jamar's right was Ana Mitchell, who was arguably the richest girl at the school. Serena began to observe her throughout the meal, and Jamar was right. Ana always picked the right fork or spoon with no hesitation at all.

"I never thought you were the type to cheat off the kid sitting next to you," she told Jamar.

"I tried to cheat off the girl on my left, but she doesn't know a teaspoon from a ladle," he said and then laughed.

Realizing he was referring to her, Serena slapped him on the arm playfully. "Sir, that is not nice!"

"I'm sorry," he said, still laughing. "I'll make it up to you."

"How?"

"I'll rent us a limo to take you home."

She rolled her eyes playfully. "You already rented a limo."

"Yeah, but I'll take you home in it," he reiterated. "I was gonna leave you here."

Serena's mouth and eyes flashed open. "Wow. I knew you were too good to be true," she joked.

"You think I'm too good to be true?" Jamar asked seriously.

Serena stared into his dark, brown eyes. "You know you are."

"No girl has ever told me that before."

"There girls you've been going out with are stupid," Serena told him.

Jamar gave that some thought before returning to his meal.

● ● ● ● ● ●

After dinner the shining couple hit the dance floor. Serena knew she was biased, but she felt like they were the most popular students in the ballroom. Jamar's friends were surprised to see him with Serena, and her friends were all curious about Jamar. The combined whirlwind of chatter kept their names buzzing like a hornet's nest.

Before he tried to bust a move, Jamar confided in his date: "I'm sorry, but I can't dance."

Serena suspected as much, but she asked, "You can't fast dance, or you can't slow dance?"

"Neither one."

"Anyone can slow dance," she said. "You just have to rock to the beat."

By then they had made their way to the outskirts of the dance floor. Serena took his hand and pulled him onto the hardwood.

"But I don't have any rhythm," Jamar complained.

"How about we just do the slow songs?" she suggested. "You can't go to the prom and not dance..."

Serena actually loved to cut a rug, but she was willing to give her dancing shoes a break tonight for Jamar's sake. She didn't want to dance with anyone other than him, and she also didn't want to do any of her *hoochie* dances while he was watching. His presence always brought out the best in her.

Jamar reluctantly followed her until she found a spot she liked, which just happened to be directly under a *Soul Train* style disco ball that hung from the ceiling. Jamar didn't bother to try more than a stiff two-step to the song that was currently playing; a heavily edited version of *No Flex Zone.*

Instead Serena danced for him. Not seductively. She took his hands as she rocked her hips and let the beat take over her body. Jamar smiled. The strobe lights swam across his face. He looked so cute. Serena smiled too, which made Jamar's heart skip a beat.

When the song ended, the DJ put on a slow jam. He told the crowd, "Alright, ladies and gentlemen. It's time to grab your date and head to the dance floor! Finley High, class of 2015, let's make some memories!"

Serena was surprised when Jamar was the one to pull her close to him for this dance. He still didn't have any moves, but he didn't need them. He wrapped his arms around his date, and she put her arms around him, and they rocked slowly. Serena rested her head on his chest and closed her eyes, and she didn't notice that the ballroom grew dim. The bright strobe lights that swam over the room dropped the red, white and yellow tints, and were now different shades of blue.

Serena would've sworn she felt Jamar's heart beat as his hand settled on the small of her back. The DJ was right; this was a memory she would never forget. This was everything she hoped it would be and more.

She always thought it was cheesy when someone described moments like this, saying they felt like it was just the two of them in the room. But it was true. Jamar made her feel like nothing and no one else mattered.

Serena grinned wistfully. She opened her eyes, and her heart stopped beating for a second when she spotted Jamar's sister Robyn standing with her friends on the outskirts of the dance floor. Robyn looked beautiful. Her dress had a sweetheart neckline. It was beige, with a beaded design on the midsection. Her hair was long and flowing. Her makeup made her look exotic.

Robyn didn't look as happy as Serena did, but that didn't mean she wasn't having a good time. The expression she wore now probably hadn't been there all night. It was caused by the evil woman her brother was clinging to on the dance floor.

But Serena's smile didn't falter. Even Robyn didn't matter right now, although she was probably the biggest threat to her and Jamar's friendship.

Serena turned Jamar casually as they danced, until Robyn was no longer in her field of view. After a moment she felt Jamar release her so he could wave at his sister, who was now facing him.

Robyn smiled and waved back, and then she turned away from them, and her smile quickly disappeared. She didn't realize she was sulking until her friend Nicole asked, "What's wrong with you?"

"Nothing," Robyn said, and her smile was back again. She walked away in search of her date.

CHAPTER TWELVE
WHISPERS

Be not fooled by the eyes, nor the lips, for the whispers
Softly slither like serpents, seducing sprite listeners
Shadowy death flickers like back drafts deprived
Of fuel, precious breaths. Souls in-tuned to the lies
Are seduced, soon consumed by these demons – know
legions
Await foolish counsel. Beasts like Satan are scheming
They're teaming with loathing. Anger-filled – for your life
Is a slap in the face. Guard your soul, child. Think twice

The prom was nearly over by the time the little pockets of chatter that seemed to follow Serena and Jamar all night began to make her feel uncomfortable. Initially she knew what her friends were thinking and saying. Jamar was a nerdy, religious type, and Serena was known to be quite the opposite. Their unlikely pairing was enough to raise quite a few eyebrows, but that was just curiosity. What Serena noticed later that night was not the same thing.

Their peers continued to sneak glances at them, but now they looked away quickly when Serena tried to make eye contact with them. Some shook their heads before they averted their attention. Serena assumed she and Jamar were garnishing these looks because some were disappointed in his choice of dates.

Out of all the good girls at the school, why did he pick **her**?

If that was the case, Serena could care less. She didn't need to live up to their expectations, and she knew that Jamar didn't care about what people had to say about him, either. But as the night wore on, she began to feel like the gossip around them was deeper than that.

She saw people whispering and watching, and she felt like she was the butt of a cruel joke. She knew it was farfetched, but she wondered if some cruel kids were planning on dumping a bucket of blood on her, like in Stephen King's famous tale.

She and Jamar were standing near the drink table with a few other friends. He was still as chipper as ever, and Serena wore a big smile for him when she said, "I'll be back in a minute."

"Okay," he said and watched as she walked away. He didn't look away until he lost track of her in the crowd.

Serena's expression was guarded as she slowly navigated the ballroom, in search of her friends. Most of the students were having a blast, and the look on their faces didn't change when Serena walked by them. But at least a dozen students had an unmistakable reaction when she looked their way. Serena knew she wasn't going crazy, so she confronted one girl who was not sitting with anyone.

"What's the problem?"

"What?" the girl said. Her name was Bethany. Serena didn't have any classes with her, but she had known her vaguely since the ninth grade.

"What are you looking at me like that for?" Serena asked her.

"I'm not... Nothing," Bethany said.

"You got something on your mind? Something you want to say?"

Serena felt her anger rising, and she heard it in her own voice, too. She didn't want to revert to her hood mentality, but she wasn't going to allow anyone to pick on her, regardless of how inadvertent it was. She wasn't going to let anyone pick on Jamar, either.

The girl continued to shake her head. She said, "I don't have anything to say," but Serena didn't believe her.

There was definitely *something* going on.

Her suspicions were confirmed when Serena finally ran into her closest friends near the dance floor. The girls were talking amongst themselves. The conversation came to an abrupt halt when Serena approached.

"Hey, what y'all doing?"

None of them responded. Serena forced a chuckle.

"Who y'all over here talking about?"

"Nobody," Toya said.

Cassandra kept her lips sealed. Cicely did as well.

Serena looked all of her friends in the eyes, one by one. Cicely was the only one who immediately looked away.

"Can I talk to you for a second?" Serena told her.

Cicely looked aghast that she would pick her. "Oh. Uh, okay," she said and reluctantly followed Serena to a more secluded part of the ballroom.

"What the hell's going on?" Serena hissed.

"I don't – what you talking about?" Cicely replied.

"You know what I'm talking about," Serena said. Her eyebrows were bunched together in a deep sneer. "I feel like people are talking about me – Toya and Cassandra included. Did you tell them something?"

They both knew there was only one thing Cicely could tell them that would result in this degree of gossiping. Serena hoped her friend hadn't betrayed her trust, but the look in Cicely's eyes made Serena's whole body freeze. Her heart started to beat hard and painfully while she waited for a response.

"Please tell me you didn't," she pleaded.

Cicely lowered her head and swallowed hard. When she looked up again, her eyes were wide and apologetic. "I'm sorry, Serena. I didn't think she would tell anybody."

Serena gasped. She let the sour breath out in shudders. The whole room went black, and there was no one but Cicely standing there. Serena hoped the blackness would consume her, too. Even before she heard the ugly truth, she wished she could simply disappear, leaving nothing behind but one of her aunt's heels for her Prince Charming to find later.

"Who did you tell?" she managed. Serena felt her hands trembling. The tremor quickly took over both of her arms and then her whole body.

"Toya," Cicely said. "I told her tonight. I don't know why I did, but I did. We was just talking. I'm sorry, Serena. I didn't think she would tell anybody."

Cicely looked genuinely regretful, but Serena didn't have any room in her heart for sympathy. If they were talking about what she thought they were talking about, then Cicely had just ruined her whole life. How does one apologize for that?

"You told her I was pregnant?"

Cicely looked like she had agreed to sell her soul to the devil as she nodded.

Serena felt a mighty wail creeping up her throat as the world opened up beneath her. She felt herself plummeting into a volcanic fissure that was surprisingly cold. The darkness enveloped her and tore her apart, and Serena welcomed death as a more favorable alternative to the pain her fleshly being was experiencing.

But when she opened her eyes, her soul reentered her body, and Cicely was still standing there. The ballroom was full, and there were smartly dressed students all around them. Serena looked around and saw that everyone was watching her now. They stared with their mouths agape. Some were smiling. Others were cursing. All were laughing and pointing.

Serena wiped the tears from her eyes and realized none of this was the case at all. But it soon would be. Her chest burned with embarrassment and regret. She couldn't breathe. She had to get out of there. But first she had to know why. Why would her best friend do this to her?

"Why did you tell her?" she cried. *"You knew she'd tell everybody!"*

"I didn't," Cicely bawled. "I swear I didn't. We're all friends. I didn't think she'd do you like that."

"She's not my friend like you are! Neither is Cassandra. *You're my best friend!"* Her voice cracked on the last word. Serena felt her tears pouring in torrents now. She quickly wiped them off her cheeks.

"She said she wouldn't tell," Cicely stated. Her eyes were wet as well.

Cicely's remorse was so poignant, Serena could taste it. But remorse wouldn't make all of her problems go away.

And even though it was Serena who had actually put herself in this predicament, she didn't feel like she was responsible for what was happening tonight. Cicely was.

"*I hate you!*" she spat before turning and walking away.

Cicely looked after her with wide, regretful eyes, but she didn't follow her.

Serena marched through the ballroom with one hand balled in a fist at her side. The other hand continued to wipe the tears that would not stop falling. Some of her classmates attempted to stop her as she stormed past them. The ones who were aware of her condition assumed the cat was finally out of the bag.

Serena didn't acknowledge any of them. She didn't stop walking until she found Jamar, who was thankfully still standing in the spot where she'd left him.

"Serena!" His heart was immediately filled with concern. "What's wrong?"

"Nothing," she said. She tried to put on a strong face for him, but it was impossible. She barely had the strength to hold her head up. She felt sick all over. She thought she might vomit.

He placed his hands on her shoulders and stared deeply into her eyes. Serena was surprised by how comforting his look and his touch was. But then she remembered that he didn't know what everyone was saying about her, and she felt even worse.

Was Cicely right all along? Had she made a fool out of Jamar by not telling him? Serena never understood how that could be the case. But now, as she looked into his eyes, she realized how naïve and innocent he was. Jamar did everything he could to make tonight perfect, and Serena ruined it all by being deceitful. She was a terrible person. She was all of the bad things people were saying about her.

"Can we please leave?" she asked, her tears coming harder now.

"Serena, tell me what happened!"

"*Please*, Jamar," she begged.

His face was a mask of concern and confusion. He said, "Yes, Serena. We can leave. Do you, did somebody do something to you? Talk to me. Please!"

Serena looked around, and her chest squeezed like a vice when she saw Robyn again. This time Jamar's sister was headed their way, with a few of her friends in tow. Unlike the first time they locked eyes tonight, Robyn no longer looked like she was hating on them for no reason. Jamar's sister still looked upset, but now her fiery brown eyes were also filled with purpose, and Serena thought she knew why.

Her mouth was so dry, she could barely speak. She tried anyway, and the words got stuck in her throat. She looked from Jamar to his sister, noting that Robyn seemed to be intent on initiating their long-awaited confrontation. Any other time Serena would've welcomed the argument and put Robyn in her place by the end of it. But not now. Not here. She turned quickly and hurried to the exit.

"I gotta go."

"Serena, wait!"

Jamar pursued her while Robyn and her entourage pursued them both.

Serena thought she had successfully escaped when she burst through the double doors and emerged in the hotel lobby, but the commotion attracted even more people. Students were drawn to her distress as bees are innately drawn to sweets, and it wasn't just Jamar who followed her into the lobby. He was the first voice she heard, though.

"Serena! Please wait!"

She reluctantly ordered her legs to stop running. There was nowhere to go. She didn't have a ride home, and her mother didn't have a car. Even if she did, Princess was still at work. Aunt Mary did have a car, but in the time it would take her to get to the hotel, Serena would be confronted by a multitude of people.

So why run? Aunt Mary once told her that what happens in the dark will ultimately come to light. The lobby of the hotel was so bright, Serena couldn't hide if she wanted to. She turned slowly and girded herself for the trauma her emotions were about to endure.

She saw Jamar first. He looked baffled, but none of the faces behind him were confused. No, they looked like they had all of the answers.

"Serena, please stop running." Seeing her distress brought tears to his eyes.

He reached for her, and then he moved quickly to ward off a blow Serena didn't even see coming. All she saw was a blur of beige dress and beautiful dark, brown hair. And then she heard screaming as Jamar fought to control his sister, who was screeching like a banshee.

"Get away from my brother, you ho!"

"Robyn, stop!"

Jamar had both of his hands on her wrists, but Robyn was nearly frantic in her pursuit. She fought to free herself, with little regard for her expensive prom dress or the fact that the sweetheart neckline was only seconds away from losing its grip on her boobs and exposing them to everyone in the lobby. Robyn looked ferocious. Nearly deranged. Her claws were extended, and they demanded blood. Serena had never seen anyone so angry at her.

"*Girl, what is your problem*?!" Jamar shouted.

He was a lot more mild-mannered and non-violent, compared to his sister. But he was bigger than her, and it was clear that this wasn't their first wrestling match. He managed to get behind her and restrain her in a powerful bear hug that also immobilized both of her arms.

Robyn began to kick at Serena wildly, using her left, then right, and then both feet. She flashed her panties to everyone standing on Serena's side of the room. But Jamar's grip was true, and there was no chance of Robyn getting away from him. Eventually she lowered both of her legs and was content with snarling at her nemesis. Serena was content with standing there and crying while more bystanders were drawn to the wild scene.

"*What is wrong with you*?!" Jamar barked next to his sister's ear. The muscles in his arms strained. His fair skin was dark with anger.

"*It's her!*" Robyn yelled. "*She's a ho, Jamar!*"

"*What? Why would – we already talked about this!*"

"*She's pregnant!*" Robyn shouted. "*Did she tell you that? That slut is pregnant!*"

The world became cold and silent again as the word **PREGNANT!** hit Serena like a wrecking ball before reverberating off of every surface in the lobby. Jamar's face went completely blank as he stared at her. Everyone in the room watched Serena with the same intensity, but she only saw Jamar.

She couldn't imagine what was going through his mind at that moment. But then again, she did know what he was thinking.

145

Whore
Slut
Liar
Freak

Even though none of these words were spoken, Serena felt them slam into her body like bullets. The trauma broke her heart and soul in two.

She watched as Jamar's grip on his sister loosened. He didn't let her go on purpose. His arms seemed to have forgotten what they were supposed to be doing, in light of the devastating bombshell his sister just delivered.

Serena thought Robyn would jump on the opportunity to exact her vengeance, but Jamar's sister didn't try to attack her again. Apparently she was satisfied with the destruction her revelation had caused.

She continued to stare at her brother's date like she was the scum of the earth until Serena turned and resumed her escape. But she didn't run this time. She slowly staggered past all of the mean faces that judged and condemned her.

Serena's gut-wrenching sobs continued to haunt the hotel lobby long after the automatic doors slid open and she disappeared into the warm, spring night.

CHAPTER THIRTEEN
SKELETONS

I can't get in contact with him
Pretty soon I'll start to show
It's been two months now
No more sign of snow
My best friend won't talk to me
Saying I'm keeping secrets

But no one can ever know

"So, I guess you don't have to tell me your secret now..."

Serena looked back and saw Jamar approaching her. She sat on a concrete bench on the outskirts of the hotel's parking lot. She would've gone further, but she thought she'd look pretty foolish if she walked the streets in her prom dress. Plus she knew Jamar would follow her, and he deserved an explanation. What he truly deserved was a girl who had maintained her sexual innocence and wouldn't make him the laughing stock of the prom. But failing that, he at least deserved an explanation.

Serena was still crying but not as hard as before. Her dried tear stains left salty, white streaks on her cheeks. Jamar thought she was a shell of her former self. Even the flower on her corsage had wilted.

He walked slowly with his hands in his pockets. Serena remained still as the click-clacking of his shoes on the asphalt grew nearer. Above them the sky was very dark. The stars scattered across the black canvas were bright and dazzling. Serena stared in her date's direction, but she didn't look up at him or make eye contact. She sat so stiffly, Jamar wasn't positive she was breathing until he saw her chest rise as she inhaled. Her shoulders were then racked by soft shudders when she exhaled.

"Can I sit down?"

She didn't respond. Jamar sat next to her, and they remained quiet for a few minutes. It was Serena who finally broke the silence.

"I'm sorry."

Her voice was soft and barely audible over the sound of cars speeding by on the main thoroughfare. Jamar tried to establish eye contact, but she continued to stare straight ahead, as if in a trance.

"Does that mean it's true?"

She nodded. A fierce grimace began to pull her cheeks down again. Jamar couldn't remember the last time he saw someone look this forlorn.

"Why didn't you tell me?"

She sniffled. She looked into his eyes, and her tears resumed their free flow. She didn't make any moves to wipe them away.

"I, I was gonna tell you," she said. "I wanted to, I wanted to wait until after prom. I didn't want to ruin the prom."

Jamar wasn't surprised by that answer. He was also not surprised by the way God laid waste to her plots and schemes. If a person's motives are not pure of heart and free from deceit, God will never bless them. It was a shame Serena had to find that out the hard way.

"You don't look pregnant," he said. "Do you know how far along you are?"

She shook her head but said, "Thr, three months. I think."

"You haven't been to the doctor?"

She shook her head again.

Jamar sighed. "Does your mother know? You haven't told anybody?"

Again Serena responded with a shake of her head. "I only told one person. To, tonight she told somebody else. Now everybody knows."

"Who's the father?" Jamar asked. "Are you still with him?"

"No." Serena searched his eyes but didn't find any of the disappointment or denouncement she expected. "I can't find him to tell him. My whole life is messed up, Jamar. I'm so sorry for dragging you into it."

"Your whole life is not messed up, Serena."

"It is, Jamar," she sobbed. "You just don't know."

"Well, tell me," he said. "Tell me everything I don't know."

Serena shook her head and watched his eyes for a long time. She was sure he couldn't offer solutions to any of her problems. And exposing all of the skeletons in her closet would probably make him hate her even more than he already did. But she needed to talk to someone who was caring and not judgmental. Her lies had already ruined their friendship, so there was no harm in coming clean at this point.

She told him about the incident with Marcus that led to an image of her breasts being seen by at least a dozen boys at school. She told him about her brief love affair with Cedric; the way he tricked her into not using a condom and how he subsequently vanished from the face of the earth.

She told him about her near-poverty level existence at home and how her mother pretty much left her to raise her brother and sisters. She told him that she had absolutely no hope for the future. And with the baby in her womb, she was destined to end up exactly like her mother.

When she was done talking, nearly fifteen minutes had passed, and she wasn't crying anymore. Jamar hadn't spoken at all during her pity party. She expected him to say, *"Yep. I've never heard of a life more messed up than yours. If you'll excuse me, I'm going back to the prom, to find a girl who isn't so jacked up."*

But he didn't say that. Instead he stood and took his suit jacket off as he walked behind her. A moment later he draped the jacket over her shoulders.

When he returned to his seat next to her, he said, "You're shivering. Are you cold?"

Serena didn't think she was, but the gesture made her feel warm and comforted. She nodded and reached to pull the jacket over her chest and midsection. She wondered why Jamar was still being so nice to her, after everything she had done to him. She didn't try to hurt him intentionally, but in the back of her mind she knew that her lie would embarrass him when he found out. Even if it didn't, it was wrong of her to treat a friend that way – especially one who was so honest and kindhearted.

Serena realized the reason he didn't respond with anger was because he was a Christian, and it was in his nature to be sympathetic to people, even if they were the lowest form of human life. That understanding broke her heart all over again, but she tried not to show it.

"Why do you say things like that?" he asked. "You know your life isn't over. You're only eighteen."

"Eighteen with a *baby*," she corrected. "Or I will be in about six months."

"A lot of women have babies when they're young," he said. "Some of them still do great things in life."

"I know Jamar. But I also know how it is where I'm from. None of the pregnant girls in my neighborhood grow up and do something great. They just get a job and try to make it. And that's what I gotta do. As soon as I graduate, I have to get a job and take care of my baby."

That was the first time she ever referred to the accident in her belly as *my baby*. It was strange, but she felt like she suddenly gained a little control over the situation, just by taking ownership.

"You probably will have to get a job," Jamar agreed. "But that doesn't mean you can't go to college. Where'd you get accepted?"

Serena looked at him like he was speaking French.

"You didn't apply to any colleges?" he asked.

She shook her head. She felt stupid again. Completely useless.

But Jamar said, "That's alright. You can start off at the community college, until you get your basics done."

She shook her head. "How am I supposed to go to college when I have a baby?"

"Girls do it all the time. They go to work and school and take care of their baby."

"I don't have any money for college."

He shrugged. "According to the republicans who are always bashing Obama, there's plenty of government assistance for minorities who want to go to school – *especially* if they have a baby."

Serena wasn't convinced. "Jamar, I know you're smart, but my grades are nowhere near good enough for college. I'm barely getting by in high school."

He grinned. "Now you're making excuses, which is something young girls in your neighborhood are good at. If you don't think you're good enough, try harder. If you're not smart enough, study more. My dad says there's nothing you can't accomplish, if you put your mind to it.

"And now you have even more of a reason to succeed in life, Serena. When your baby gets here, he needs to know that his mom is willing to do whatever it takes to get him in a nice home; hopefully one with a Christian husband at the helm."

Serena knew that everything he said was true. His mention of her future husband made her wonder where he fit into the picture. She knew that she was falling in love with him, but she felt like it was a mistake. There was no way they could ever be together. To believe anything different would be foolish.

"I guess you don't want to go back inside," he said.

Serena shook her head. It was going to be hard enough to face her peers at school on Monday. She certainly didn't want to do it now, while the incident was still fresh on everyone's mind.

Jamar checked his watch. "Our ride won't be here for thirty more minutes. But I can call and tell him to come early."

Serena's eyes narrowed. "Our ride?"

"The limo," he said. "I know you didn't forget about our limo."

"No. I didn't. But I didn't think you'd want to take me home in it, after what happened."

"I already paid to have it until one a.m.," he explained. "It's only ten-thirty. We actually don't have to go straight home, if you don't want to..."

Serena was even more perplexed by that. "What do you mean?"

"Isn't there supposed to be a lot of after-prom parties tonight? You don't want to go to any of them?"

"I... I didn't think you would," she said. "I mean, even before what happened tonight. I didn't think that was your kind of crowd, with all the drinking and sex and stuff..."

"Oh, no. You're right, that's not my crowd. But I don't mind going, if you want to. We can still hang out *without drinking* can't we?"

Serena hesitated.

"Come on, this is prom night," he said with a grin. "I don't want your prom to be ruined because of what my sister did."

"But what about you?" Serena wondered. "What about what I did to you? I can't believe you want to be seen with me."

"What am I supposed to do? Unfriend you?" he joked. "This isn't Facebook. I don't even know how that would work in real life."

But Serena was serious. "All you have to do is not talk to me anymore. Problem solved."

"I'm not going to abandon you because you have a problem," he said. "I don't care what anyone else has to say about it. Anyone who would make fun of you or talk down to you because you're pregnant is not my friend. The bible says judge not, lest ye be judged."

Serena was aware of that passage, but she had never met anyone who took it to heart like Jamar did. It was a beautiful thing. Surreal, even.

"I don't want to go to any of those parties," she told him. "I know I'm going to have to deal with all of their questions, and I don't want to do it tonight. I've had enough stress."

"I understand," Jamar said. Then, "I've got an idea of where we can go."

Serena couldn't believe it, but she was actually getting excited again. "Where?"

"I'm not telling you," he said. "I want to surprise you."

Serena smiled. Jamar's continuous acts of kindness made her heart flutter.

"Okay," she said, "as long as you promise there won't be any students from our school there."

"I can't promise that," he said. "I have no idea where all of our classmates are going. But I can promise that it's not one of their parties, and it's not a destination anyone at the prom is talking about. And I promise to keep you safe."

Serena's interest was definitely piqued then. "Okay," she said. "I'll go."

"Great."

Jamar dug his cellphone from his pocket and called the limo company. He told them he and his date were ready to leave the prom. While they waited for the driver to arrive, he surprised Serena by putting his arm around her. She told herself that he only did that because he thought she was cold. But she couldn't stop her heart from hoping it meant something more.

She leaned into his embrace and thought about how happy she'd been with him on the dance floor. Jamar was right: It would be a tragedy to let Robyn ruin what had been such a magical night. She couldn't wait to see the surprise he had in store for her.

CHAPTER FOURTEEN
ONE WISH

Sweet angel, your spirit so gently caresses
My essence. Your presence speaks softly. The nexus
Of my state of mind, sweet divine, you're the reason
For light, precious raindrops, the seasons. I believe in
True joy, for your kiss brings me happiness. Your smile
Warms my soul. Your touch births quick tremors

The second ride in the limo was as nice as the first.
Serena was more comfortable, so she spent a lot of time
checking out all of the electronic gadgets that were at their
disposal. She found an old school R&B station on the radio,
and they listened to Luther Vandross and New Edition while
the luxury car rolled so smoothly, Serena could barely tell
they were moving.

When they got downtown, Jamar pushed a button
that allowed him to communicate with the driver up front.

"Can you drop us off at 6th and Houston?" he asked
over the intercom.

"Yes sir," the driver said. "How long will you be
there?"

"A couple of hours."

"It's going to be hard to find somewhere for me to park downtown," the driver complained. "I'll have to find a valet."

"That's fine."

"Valet parking a limo is more expensive than a car..."

"Don't worry. I got you," Jamar told him.

Serena gave him a look, but she didn't know anything about his arrangements with the limo company, so she kept her mouth closed.

When the driver pulled to a stop at the designated intersection, he got out to open the door for the teenagers. Jamar produced an impressive fold of twenty dollar bills and peeled off two of them.

"This should cover your parking," he said as he handed over the first one. "And you can get yourself something to eat while you wait on us." He offered the other twenty to pay for the driver's meal.

"Thank you, sir." The money quickly disappeared into the man's pocket.

As they walked away, Serena said, "You know he's probably going to keep that money and find somewhere to park that limo for free. He might buy a bag of chips and a soda."

"Probably," Jamar agreed.

"You're okay with that?"

"Tonight I am. I want everything to be perfect for us, from here on out."

Serena knew that he was referring to the rest of their date being perfect rather than the rest of their lives together, but she couldn't stop her heart from sighing.

"Everything is perfect," she told him. "I appreciate everything you've done."

They smiled at each other as the limo driver returned to his seat and slowly rolled away. Jamar reached and took hold of her hand. Serena thought he was going to kiss her. She hoped he would, with all her heart. But he turned and looked down the busy street instead.

"Are you hungry?"

"Not really," Serena said, hoping her disappointment over the would be/could be kiss didn't show.

"Do you want something light?" he asked. "What about sushi?"

"I never had that before."

Jamar was stunned. "You've never had sushi?"

"I don't eat out much," she revealed. "And Mama never made it at home."

"Well, tonight you should experience it," Jamar said, and he started walking towards one of the brightly lit restaurants in the area.

Serena strolled casually beside him. They continued to hold hands. It was getting late, but the downtown traffic was nearly bumper to bumper. The sidewalks were filled with other couples who all seemed to notice how elegantly Jamar and Serena were dressed.

A street vendor even asked him, "Is today prom night?"

"Yes," Jamar said with a grin.

"Y'all have fun. And be *good*," the vendor said with a not-so-casual wink that said they should definitely be *naughty* tonight rather than good.

Serena blushed a little, but Jamar seemed oblivious to the innuendo.

He told him, "We will, sir. Thanks!"

● ● ● ● ● ●

They went to P.F. Chang's, which was a lot more expensive than Serena anticipated. She was reluctant to order anything, but Jamar was quite insistent.

"It's prom night. And we're both seniors, so this is the only one we'll ever get."

"That doesn't mean you have to spend fifty bucks on me."

"Oh, I've spent way more than that, if you want to get technical."

He was smiling, but Serena really didn't want to be a burden. "That doesn't mean you have to spend fifty *more* dollars at this restaurant."

"Come on," he urged her. "You said you've never had sushi. I want you to experience it for the first time, with me."

Serena couldn't turn down that offer if she wanted to. There were a lot of things she wanted to experience with Jamar.

"Okay."

"Great," he said, picking up his menu. "What kind do you want? Octopus?"

"Oh God, no."

"If I order octopus, will you at least try it."

She considered it and said, "Okay."

"I noticed you always say no at first, and then give in when I push."

Serena's face heated. "You noticed that?"

"Yeah," he said. "Got me wondering what else I can push for."

Now Serena felt the heat in her chest and in her belly.

"Don't worry," he said, still smiling. "I would never violate your virtue in any way."

"I know you wouldn't."

They stared at each other for a while. Serena hoped he'd continue the conversation; maybe add a "*But*..." to his last comment. But he didn't.

"I'm also getting shark," he said, returning to his menu. "I think you should get something exotic, too."

"Yes, I think I will," she said and lifted her own menu.

● ● ● ● ● ●

When they left the restaurant it was nearly midnight. Serena was full and happy and caught up in the magic of the night. After what happened at the prom, she knew that most girls would have gone home and cried into their pillow. It was clear that Jamar was doing everything he could to make sure the incident with his sister became nothing more than a side note, rather than the focal point of their prom.

It was a small gesture, but to Serena it was huge. It felt awesome to know that Jamar truly cared about her, and he would never intentionally hurt her – unlike her exes Marcus and Cedric, who probably never cared for her at all.

As they walked hand-in-hand on the now sparsely populated sidewalk, Serena wished there was something she could do to show her appreciation for everything Jamar had done for her. She didn't know where their lives would take them after tonight. She hoped he would remain in her life, so she could at least try to make it up to him.

When they continued to stroll past the intersection the driver dropped them off at, she asked, "Where are we going now?"

"Somewhere pretty," he said vaguely.

Curiosity was getting the best of her, but Serena didn't ask any more questions. She knew his destination would be a pleasant one, whatever it was.

Ten minutes later his surprise was revealed when they entered the Water Gardens, which was one of Overbrook Meadows' biggest downtown attractions. Growing up in the city, Serena had been there quite a few times, but never at night. Back in the day, there were rumors that hobos took over the park after sunset and made it dangerous for tourists. But the police started a new initiative a few years ago to fight back against the vagrants. Thanks to them, the area was now safe twenty four hours a day.

The Water Gardens was an architectural and engineering masterpiece that featured pools, fountains, slopes, hills and even complex valleys; all made of concrete and all flowing with water. Even some of the walls enclosing tight corridors had an endless flow of water running down them.

The park was well-lit, and Serena noticed something else she had never seen during her previous visits: All of the exhibits had different color lights that tinted the spurting water blue and yellow and red and green. Her heart was enraptured by the perfectly manufactured beauty from the moment they followed a cobblestone trail into the watery paradise.

She told Jamar, "This is beautiful! Thanks for bringing me here."

He smiled, and they continued to stroll leisurely, like newlyweds.

After thirty minutes of star, moon and water gazing, they arrived at the Pool of Tranquility. Unlike other areas of the park, the water here was still, with no fountains or streams or anything else that would make a sound. The water in the pool was turquoise. There was at least twenty dollars' worth of coins at the bottom of the pool, which was another reason vagrants once considered this place a gold mine.

Serena found a quarter in her clutch purse. She made a wish and flipped the coin in the air. She and Jamar watched until it created a slight splash on the surface of the water before sinking to the bottom of the pool.

"What'd you wish for?" he asked.

"I'm not telling you."

"You know what I wish?" he said.

Serena had no idea. She shook her head.

"I wish I had more courage," he told her.

"Why do you say that?"

"I wanted to defend you more, when my sister tried to attack you at the prom. But I always think of the best stuff to say afterwards."

Serena giggled. It felt good to laugh rather than cry about what happened. "What did you want to say?"

"I wanted to tell everyone who was watching to worry about their own problems, before they get involved with someone else's. Let he who is without sin cast the first stone."

Serena's eyes widened. She laughed. "You were going to tell them that in the middle of that fight?"

He nodded. "Yep. But I didn't think of it until later."

Serena laughed again as she imagined how that would've played out. She could see Jamar standing tall in the midst of the conflict, like Moses, ordering the bystanders to leave his date alone.

"You defended me just fine," she said.

"Did I?"

She nodded and then did a curtsy. "My hero."

He chuckled. "So your prom wasn't ruined?"

"No. Not at all. You made everything perfect."

"Not quite," he said. "There is one more prom tradition we missed..."

Serena had a lot of thoughts about what that could be, but none of those ideas seemed appropriate for Jamar. She didn't have time to ask what he was referring to before he approached her slowly and took hold of her hands again. Serena looked up at him with a smile as he closed the distance between them. Overhead the moon was bold and bright.

Serena thought he was moving in for a hug, but Jamar surprised her by inching his face closer to hers. By the time their lips touched, her heart was knocking like a jackhammer. It was not like her to get so excited over a little kiss, but she knew this was much more than that.

Jamar's lips were soft and warm. He pecked her hesitantly at first. Serena squeezed his hands, and he deepened the kiss. He let go of her hands, and his arms moved to embrace her. Serena nearly swooned when she felt his hand on her side. The other settled on the small of her back.

He pulled her closer to him. When their bodies pressed together, a quivery sigh escaped her lips. Jamar's grip on her body tightened. He kissed her again, taking a moment to briefly suck her bottom lip before he mercifully released her.

Serena's head swam in a pool of perfect bliss. She didn't open her eyes for another three seconds. When she did, Jamar stood sheepishly, glowing as radiantly as the stars above. Serena knew that she would never forget this moment, the look in his eyes, no matter where life led them in the days and months and years to come.

• • • • • •

On the way back to the projects, Serena got a chance to fulfill another one of her wishes. Jamar opened the sunroof on the limo, and she took her heels off and stood on the sofa. She was so high at that point, she got nearly her whole torso out of the sunroof. It was the perfect, thrilling end to an awesome night.

She spread her arms wide and screamed at the stars, *"I'm on top of the world*!" which Jamar found quite amusing.

Another thing Jamar found interesting was her long, sexy legs and the beautiful curves of Serena's hips and butt, which were eye-level to him as she stood on the sofa. He felt guilty for looking, even though he wasn't touching. But from a logistical standpoint, he *had* to keep an eye on her, to make sure she didn't fall.

Yeah, he told himself, *any excuse will do.*

Jamar knew that a lot of people thought he wasn't interested in sex because he chose to abstain. But that wasn't the case at all. At his age, it was impossible not to have certain urges.

The only thing that kept him sane was God's promise that his lovemaking would be much more glorious if he waited until marriage. That was a promise worth waiting for. Jamar knew there would be just as much temptation in college as there was in high school – probably even more so.

But his faith never failed to keep him strong, especially at times like this, when his flesh was so weak.

When Serena returned to her seat, her hair was windblown, and her eyes were watery from the wind in her face.

"That was so awesome!" she exclaimed. "You should see how beautiful everything is!"

"I did," Jamar replied. "And I agree. Everything is very beautiful."

CHAPTER FIFTEEN
THE FINAL CHAPTER
THE AFTERMATH

Robyn made it home at 1:28 a.m. She blew out a sigh of relief when she entered and found the living room completely dark. But her relief was short-lived. After closing and locking the front door, she turned and was startled by a dark figure on the loveseat. The person stood to his full, imposing height, and as Robyn's eyes adjusted to the darkness, she realized it was her father.

Stephen's head moved slowly towards the clock mounted above the entertainment center. Despite the darkness, he could make out the position of the big hand and the little hand.

"Barely made it," he said in a deep voice that sent chills down Robyn's spine.

Her throat was stiff with anxiety. She panted softly but didn't respond.

"How was your night?" he asked.

Robyn's pulse raced. Her eyes were as big as silver dollars. "It, it was fine," she replied.

166

"I'm glad it's over," Stephen said honestly. "Prom night may be fun for you guys, but it's a big headache for me and your mom. I couldn't sleep until I knew you were home safe."

He stepped to her suddenly. Robyn squeezed her eyes closed. She knew he was going to confront her about the incident with Serena. But her dad simply kissed her on the forehead before turning and heading down the hallway.

"Goodnight," he called over his shoulder.

"Goodnight," Robyn told him.

She waited a few seconds to make sure he wasn't coming back to yell at her after all, but he didn't. Confused, Robyn continued down the hallway and stopped at her brother's room. The door was open, but she knocked anyway before entering.

A form huddled under the blankets on the bed told her, "Come in."

Robyn entered the rcom hesitantly and took a seat on the corner of the bed. Jamar sat up and stared at her. He was only wearing a tee shirt and boxers under the blankets. Robyn was still in her full prom attire. They watched each other for a while. She looked supremely unsure of herself, and Jamar was fine with letting her stew in those juices.

"You didn't tell Dad?" she finally asked.

He shook his head slowly.

Robyn couldn't believe he passed up an opportunity to get her in trouble. "Why not?"

He shrugged. "I don't hate you, Robyn."

"I, I know you don't. But I know you're mad at me."

He surprised her by saying, "I'm not even mad at you."

"You, where'd you go after the prom?"

"We went downtown," he said. "We went out to eat and then to the Water Gardens."

Robyn frowned. "But what about – did she tell you she wasn't pregnant?"

"No, she is pregnant," Jamar confirmed.

"You're not mad at her for lying to you?"

"If I got pregnant in high school, I don't think I'd run around telling everybody, either."

"But she played you."

"No, she didn't. I asked her to go the prom with me, and she said yes. I didn't need to know that she was pregnant. I still would've taken her if I knew."

"But why? Why would you want to go out with some pregnant hoodrat?"

"Really?" Jamar said. "After all the trouble you caused tonight, you still wanna call her names?"

"Alright, fine. Why would you want to go out with a pregnant girl?"

"Because people make mistakes," he said. "And I'm not in a position to judge anyone. Let he who is without sin cast the first stone. I meant to tell you that at the hotel, but I didn't think of it in time."

Robyn shook her head in disbelief. "So you still like her?"

"How can you sit there and talk like you're better than her?" Jamar wondered.

"I didn't say I was better than her."

"Well, what do you think you're doing? You try to fight that girl because she's pregnant–"

"No. I wanted to slap the crap out of her because she lied, and she's using my brother."

"But I just told you she didn't use me. I'm the one who asked her to go to the prom. She didn't ask me."

"Jamar, I don't get you."

"That's because your heart is cold, and you need to figure out a way to open it up," he suggested.

"You think I'm cold?"

"Yes, Robyn. Sometimes."

"I was only trying to look out for you."

"That's another thing," Jamar said. "I'm eighteen. You're seventeen. I'm the big brother. I don't need you to look out for me so much."

"But you're too nice," she complained. "Sometimes I think you're so religious, you don't see the problems in the real world. People take advantage of you."

"If that's the case, then you should let me learn my lesson on my own. I'll never be able to make it in the real world, if you're always trying to shield me from harm."

"I only do it because I love you."

"And you know I love you too, Robyn. But sometimes you're wrong. Like tonight. Why don't you put yourself in Serena's shoes for a second?"

She shook her head in dismissal, but her brother kept talking.

"Imagine you're eighteen, and you messed up and got pregnant by some boy who's not even around anymore. You're too scared to tell your mom, and you don't want anyone at school to find out either. You grew up poor, so you know how this story goes: You get out of high school, you have your baby, you get a job, and that's it. You get on welfare, and you end up having more babies with more guys you aren't married to.

"But before all of that happens, a guy asks you to go to the prom. And for one night in your entire life, you get to experience something that's not supposed to be in your plans. You get to wear a pretty dress and ride in a limo and be *normal*. Everybody deserves to have that. But you almost robbed Serena. She never did anything to hurt you or me. She didn't deserve what you did, and you owe her an apology."

He didn't think his sister would absorb any of that, but she surprised him by lowering her head and sighing.

"Alright. I guess you got a point."

Jamar knew that was the closest she would ever come to apologizing, so he let it go. Hopefully she would take his words to heart and treat people better in the future.

"How did everything go with Tony?" he asked, referring to her prom date.

Robyn's smile came back immediately. "It was awesome!"

"You didn't go to his house afterwards?" Jamar asked. "Or to the mo' mo'."

Her eyes widened. "What's the mo' mo'?"

"The motel."

She laughed. "How do you know about that?"

"I may not participate, but I'm a great listener."

"No, I didn't go home with him," Robyn said. "*Or to the mo' mo'.*" She laughed again. "I'm not having sex until I get married. I don't care if it is prom night. Daddy would kill me."

"I would, too," Jamar said. "And then I'd have to kill your boyfriend."

She gave him a doubtful look.

"Hey, I'll always be your big brother," he told her. "And big brother don't play that!"

• • • • • •

Serena was still awake when her mother came home from work at two a.m. She waited until Princess took a shower and got ready for bed before she entered her bedroom with Annie in her arms. Princess smiled at the sight of her baby. She reached for her and hugged her affectionately when Serena handed her over.

"How was prom?"

Serena sat on the bed with a huge smile on her face. She was already dressed for bed in a nightgown and slippers.

"It was *amazing*."

"Really? You didn't do anything bad afterwards, did you?"

Serena shook her head, and then her smile faded. She brought her hands together over her stomach and said, "Mama, I gotta tell you something."

"What?" Princess said. "That you're pregnant?"

Serena's eyes widened. Her mouth fell open as well.

Princess frowned and nodded. "Girl, I already knew. Been waiting to see how long you'd go before you told me."

"But, but how?"

"I'm your mother," Princess said. "Why did you think I wouldn't figure it out?"

Serena shook her head in confusion.

"I know you been throwing up in the morning," Princess said. "This house is way too small to keep something like that a secret. And I know you was real upset when you broke up with that boy a few months ago. What was his name – Cedric?"

Serena nodded, her eyes still wide with amazement.

"The way you was carrying on, crying all up and down the street, I could tell it was more than just a regular breakup," Princess said. "And then you started going to church all of a sudden. I figured that was a good thing, either way. But going to church right after that breakup told me it was something really wrong that you ain't had no way to fix by yourself.

"But the *biggest* piece of the puzzle came when I was looking for some papers I threw away a while back, must'a been two months ago," Princess said. "I found your pregnancy test. I didn't find the stick, just the box it came in. I put all of that together, and it solved the mystery."

Serena couldn't have been more astonished. She forgot that street smarts can be as important as book smarts sometimes.

"How far along are you?" her mother asked.

Serena shook her head. "I don't know. If it happened when I think it did, I'm three months."

"What the doctor say? You doing alright?"

Serena shook her head again.

"Girl, you been to the doctor, ain't you?"

Serena continued to shake her head, and now her eyes filled with tears as well. When she met her mother's eyes, the tears began to stream down her face.

"Aww, baby." Princess got up from her spot on the bed and moved closer to her. "Why you crying?"

"Because, because my life is over," Serena bawled. "I didn't even make it out of high school without getting pregnant."

"That's okay, honey. It's not the end of the world."

It's not the end of the world?

Serena thought she got a boost of confidence from Jamar, but looking into her mother's eyes made her feel like she was staring at a future version of herself.

"*Yes it is.* I wanted to go to college and do something with my life. Now I'm stuck. I won't never get out of here, these projects."

"Serena, you know that's not true. You can still do whatever you want to."

"How, Mama? How am I supposed to go to school with a baby? How am I supposed to get a job? I can't do nothing but get on welfare."

"What? Girl, that's just straight up foolishness. Where you learn that from?"

Serena stared at her mother but was unable to point a finger at her.

"Me?" Princess said. "That's what I taught you?"

Again Serena didn't feel comfortable confirming that.

"Listen," her mother said. "Everybody ain't the same. Yes, I have four children with no man around, and I don't have an awesome job or a car. But that don't mean that's the life for you, girl. You're way smarter than me, Serena. And you don't hate school like I did.

"When I got out, I never wanted to see another book again in my life. But you got goals that require some college, and you can make it. It ain't that hard. It's plenty of pregnant women at the college."

That was the second time Serena heard that tonight, so she knew it must be true.

"But I won't have anybody to watch the baby when I go to school and stuff."

Princess frowned. "What do you think I am? A ghost or something?"

"Mama, you need me to watch *your* kids all the time. You're always too busy."

"Serena, I know I depend on you a lot, but that's what families are for. When you need help with your baby, I'll be there for you. And your Aunt Mary will be there. And pretty soon Paul will be there for you, too. Your grandmother only stays fifteen minutes away. There's plenty of people here for you, baby. All you got to do is ask for help. And quit keeping secrets."

Serena was surprised by the direction of this conversation. Her mother had never shown this level of support. Serena had always felt like Princess' children were at the bottom of her priority list. She didn't have high hopes of Princess giving up her current lifestyle by the time the baby arrived, but it felt good to know that her mother promised to be there for her.

"I'm sorry, Mama. I guess I was just scared."

"Of course you're scared," Princess said. "You're eighteen and pregnant and don't want nobody to know about it. That would scare the hell out of anybody!"

They laughed and Serena leaned in for a big hug when her mother threw her arm around her. She was still holding Annie, so the baby was in the midst of the embrace, too.

Serena looked down at her little sister and decided her family was kind of awesome. They didn't have a lot, but they always shared what they had. No one ever had to go without something essential. And Princess may appear to be a little too carefree at times, but she worked full time and made sure all four of her children were healthy and provided for.

Serena concluded that she would much rather have a poor family like hers that was full of love, rather than one of those rich families where everyone stayed in their rooms and hated each other.

● ● ● ● ● ●

She went to sleep that night thinking about the prom, hoping to steer her dreams in that direction.

When she woke up the next morning, Serena didn't remember anything that played out in her subconscious mind while she slumbered. But her lips felt warm and tender, and Jamar's sweet kiss was the first thing on her mind.

For the next thirty minutes, nothing could wipe the smile off her face – not even diaper duty with her little sister Annie.

EPILOGUE

It's been three months
It's really hard to hide
I have to get help,
But from where?
For so long I've tried...
"Mom, I have to tell you—"
"Girl, I know you're pregnant
You can't keep secrets
Why haven't you told me yet?"

Someone finally knows

By Jasmine Walker

Returning to school on Monday after the prom proved to be as stressful as Serena expected. Her scandal was the biggest story on campus. It wasn't long before even the freshmen were pointing and snickering at Serena behind her back.

If that wasn't bad enough, she felt like she didn't have anyone to turn to for support. Her best friend Cicely was the one who ratted her out, and her other best friend Toya was responsible for igniting the gossip. Serena felt like she couldn't trust or confide in anyone – except Jamar. But he was a victim of the rumor mill, too. The students were convinced he was duped into caring for an obvious sinner. But at least that story generated sympathy for him.

Serena, on the other hand, was deemed to be wicked and evil. It was hard to keep her head up, when it felt like every set of eyes in the hallways were watching and convicting her. By lunchtime she wanted to flee the school. She didn't simply want to skip the rest of the day. She wanted to drop out altogether, so she wouldn't have to deal with the consequences of her deceit. If it wasn't for Jamar, she might have actually done it.

He stopped by her locker at the end of third period. Serena's heart began to beat slowly and sickly at the sight of him.

"Hey," he said.

"Hey."

"You coming to the meeting?"

Serena knew the bible club met on Mondays and Fridays, but she was surprised that he asked.

"I, I wasn't planning on it."

"How come?"

"I was trying to give you some space," she told him. "People are already talking about us. I don't want them to think we're going out. It will make it worse, for you."

He smiled. "People have been talking about me since the seventh grade. That's nothing new."

"Yeah, but that was because you're so religious. Now they're talking about what happened between you and me."

"Serena, you should know I don't care about stuff like that. As long as I know who I am in my heart, and God knows it too, it doesn't matter what anybody else thinks."

"I wish I could be that sure of myself."

"Come to the meeting," he said. "We need to talk about this, as a group. And we need to pray for you."

"Jamar–"

"God said that when two or more people come together in His name, He will be in the midst. You can't rely on your classmates to make you feel better, because most of them are idiots. You have to find the strength inside of *you*. God can help you with that."

Her eyes filled with tears. She didn't think she was this emotional before she got pregnant.

"Come to the meeting," Jamar pleaded. "Let us help you."

So she did.

• • • • • •

On Tuesday the rabble-rousers were still stirring the pot. And now they felt comfortable enough to approach Serena directly with their questions and suppositions.

Are you and Jamar going out?

Did you and Jamar have sex?

I heard you lied to Jamar about being pregnant.

Are you pregnant with Jamar's baby?

Who's your baby-daddy?

Are you going to get an abortion?

I heard you had a baby at the prom and left it in the bathroom.

Serena didn't want to entertain any of this foolishness, but she knew that rumors at school could only maintain their sensationalism if the theories were more interesting than the truth. So she answered their questions one by one, hoping her run-of-the-mill pregnancy would be deemed boring, compared to other things going on at the school.

Tuesday was also the day Serena's friends sought her out at lunchtime. Serena got her tray and tried to find an empty table in the cafeteria, but there were at least two people seated at all of them.

She sat with a few juniors she didn't know and tried to be inconspicuous as she gnawed on a slice of pizza that wasn't half bad. She looked up from her lunch when her three friends suddenly approached and sat around her; two in front and one on her right.

"What's up? You don't wanna kick it with us no more?" Toya asked.

Serena glared at her. She inhaled angrily, causing her nostrils to flare.

"I'm sorry I told her you were pregnant," Cicely said. "For real, Serena. I didn't think she would tell anybody."

"I can't apologize for telling people, 'cause y'all know I got a big mouth," Toya stated.

Cassandra remained quiet. Serena did, too.

"So what that mean?" Toya said. "You still mad at us?"

"Yes, I'm mad," Serena said. "Everybody at school is talking about me."

"They always talking about something," Toya said. "You ain't special. They'll move on to somebody else sooner or later."

Serena sighed roughly. She put her pizza down and scowled at Toya.

"What do I have to do to make it up to you?" Cicely asked.

"I wanna make it up, too," Toya said. "Tell us what you want us to do."

Serena was surprised to hear that from her. Toya was rarely apologetic. It was even more uncommon for her to want to make amends for something she did wrong.

"I don't want anything," Serena said. "It's too late to do anything."

"No it's not," Cicely said. "We can help you."

"Yeah," Toya agreed. "A lot of people are talking noise about you, but I tell them to shut up every time I hear it."

"I do too," Cicely said.

"And if you hang out with us," Toya went on, "instead of trying to be by yourself, we can make sure people know that if they mess with you, they have to go through all of us."

Serena looked her friends in the eyes one by one, and she decided that might actually help the situation. Bullies preyed on the weak and the defenseless. They rarely went after someone who had an entourage ready to protect them.

"Alright," she said. "That's fine."

"Cool," Toya said. "So, um, what did Jamar have to say about your, um, your baby?"

Serena shook her head, but she also smiled. Her friends weren't necessarily great people, but she loved them, and she knew that deep down they had her best interests in mind.

"I told him his sister was lying about me being pregnant. I still haven't told him the truth," she joked.

"What?" Toya's eyes widened. "Girl, you better hurry up! Everybody knows about it. You know I can't keep secrets. I'll probably end up telling him myself!"

● ● ● ● ● ●

By the end of the week Serena's story had lost most of its flair, and she was comfortable with her predicament. She also found that she was not alone. There was a girl named Leticia who was seven months pregnant and five more seniors who were in their first trimester. There was even a sophomore who was showing already and a freshman who was rumored to have had an abortion.

The following week an even bigger scandal hit the school, and Serena's story was all but forgotten: One of the teachers got arrested at the beginning of first period. Everyone at the school had a different guess as to why the arrest was made and why it was done so publicly. Serena had to wait until she got home and watched the news to get any concrete information.

According to the reporter, Mrs. Chestnut had inappropriate sexual relations with at least one of her students. They didn't mention the student's name, but they indicated there was photographic evidence of the alleged encounter.

At school the next day everyone wanted to play Sherlock Holmes and figure out who the student was. Serena was one of few people who avoided the gossip.

"That ain't none of my business."

● ● ● ● ● ●

Later that month all of the seniors at Finley High were excited about graduation. None of Serena's close friends got scholarships to any university, but Cicely got a grant that would help her go to TCU, and Cassandra got accepted to Texas Lutheran.

When asked how she would finance such an expensive education, Cassandra said, "My mom says I can get a student loan, and I don't have to pay it back until after I graduate and get a job."

When she got home from school that day, Serena asked her mother if she should follow in her friend's footsteps.

"Don't do it," her mother advised. "You know your Aunt Mary is still paying off her student loan, and she didn't do nothing but go to a trade school. She started off owing six thousand, and now they say it's twelve thousand!

"Just go to the community college, like you're planning on, and let them help you with as much financial aid as you can get. I ain't saying you should use the system, but you're black, and you finna have a baby. There's programs that will help you, girl. You probably won't have to pay for nothing – not even your books."

Serena was against using state and government aid like that, but it sounded a lot better than having to pay back a student loan after she graduated. Plus she didn't plan on misusing the funds, like so many other women in her neighborhood. She only wanted to better herself, so that she could become independent as quickly as possible.

"Okay," she said. "Will you help me fill out the applications?"

"Yeah, girl. I'm off on Thursday. We can go down there when you get out of school."

● ● ● ● ● ●

Serena graduated on May 29th, 2015. She wasn't at the top of her class, but she was happy to say she wasn't at the bottom, either. She was more than three months pregnant by then. She was barely showing, and you couldn't see her baby bulge underneath her graduation gown.

Her family took her out for dinner after the ceremony. Aunt Mary came with her husband and her children, and Serena's grandmother was there, too.

Serena was the first one of Princess' brood to walk across the stage. Apparently that was a big deal. Serena didn't think so at the time. But years later, after watching her brother Paul struggle with crime and expulsion in high school, she realized her diploma did mean a lot.

"What you wanna do when you get out of college?" her grandmother asked over a huge plate of fried and broiled shrimp.

"I wanna be a nurse," Serena told her.

"That's good," her granny said. "We'll always need nurses, and I know you like to help people."

"I'm so proud of you!" Aunt Mary said.

"Me, too," Princess agreed. "Serena always been the smart one."

Serena considered that statement ironic, considering she was currently with child. But her family wanted to dote on her that night, and she didn't have a problem letting them.

"You gon' get a desert?" her mother asked.

Serena was already full from her entrée, and she knew the prices at Red Lobster were probably higher than her family could afford.

"You might as well," Princess said. "Ain't no telling when we'll be able to come back here."

"Alright," Serena said and picked up the desert menu.

"Can I get a desert?" her little brother Paul asked.

"Naw boy!" Princess snapped. "You ain't graduated nothing!"

• • • • • •

During the summer break, Serena and Jamar went out a couple of times, but it was never the same as it was on prom night. They never hugged or held hands, and it became clear that the romance they shared when she wore her purple dress was not a permanent thing.

Serena was heartbroken at first, but over time she came to understand and accept their situation. Jamar was travelling to Lubbock to study engineering at Texas A&M. He was still very deep in the bible, and he was still a virgin. If he was interested in having a girlfriend, he didn't show it. He was always polite, though. And he never made Serena feel uncomfortable about her protruding belly.

After much soul-searching, she decided that they were two comets on completely different paths. They collided once, and it was bright and beautiful, but it didn't alter their courses. She knew Jamar would grow up and marry a beautiful woman who loved the Lord as much as he did. They would have plenty of babies, and Jamar would be the head of a strong, Christian household.

By the end of summer, Serena stopped hoping she would be that woman. But she would never stop caring for him. Prom night would be the highlight of her life for years to come. She made a photo album from all of the pictures she collected, and she flipped through it sometimes. The trip down memory lane inevitably brought her to tears, but they weren't sad tears. Not always.

• • • • • •

In August Serena started school at Overbrook Meadows Community College. Her mother was right; she didn't have to pay for anything, not even her books. She was so far along in her pregnancy at that point, it looked like she had a basketball stuffed under her shirt. But Serena never felt ostracized. Most of her classmates were young, but there were students at the college from all walks of life. No one saw anything wrong with another pregnant adult.

Within the first week of school, all of Serena's professors inquired about her due date and began to make arrangements for her to continue her course work after she had the baby. Some of her tests and assignments could be completed online, and they were willing to extend the due dates for any work that wasn't.

Serena didn't expect things to go so smoothly. She was still attending church regularly, and she said her prayers almost on a daily basis. She gave God all of the credit for helping her through the transition from high school to college. She knew that she could do nothing without Him.

• • • • • •

Crystal Lynette Massey was born on Saturday, November 14th. Serena fell in love with her the moment the nurse placed the baby in her arms.

By then Serena had learned the whereabouts of Crystal's father. Cedric was serving three to five years in the same penitentiary as Serena's father. Patrick offered to find Cedric and exact vengeance for the way he ran out on her, but Serena quickly vetoed that.

The only thing she wanted was to continue school, so that she could provide a good life for her daughter. Cedric would have to deal with his shortcomings on his own. Serena didn't think she would ever even file for child support.

● ● ● ● ● ●

Jamar called a few times during their first semester of college. He called again in December. This time Serena was happy to see his home phone number on the Caller ID.

"Hey! You're at home?"

"Yeah. I came back for Christmas break."

"That's cool. I'm glad you called."

"How's that baby?"

"She's fine." Serena sat on her bed with a wide grin on her face. "How's school?"

"It gets tough sometimes," Jamar said. "I like living on campus, but I miss my friends and family. Can I, is it alright if I come see you?"

"Yeah. That would be great. When?"

"Right now."

Serena didn't think she'd have time to get dolled-up for him, but she could never refuse his request. "Okay. You know where I stay..."

Jamar knocked on her door twenty minutes later. Serena answered wearing jeans and a tee shirt. Jamar wore khakis with a golf shirt that was tucked in neatly. He had only been gone for four months, but Serena thought he looked different, more mature. His hair was trimmed short and neat, but he had a slight moustache now as well as a tuft of hair on his chin.

Overall, she thought he was gorgeous, more so than the night they went to the prom. He smiled at her, and she threw her arms around him, pulling him into a tight hug. He hugged her back, just as tightly.

She invited him inside, and they chatted for an hour about school, family and their college experiences. Crystal was asleep the whole time, but that didn't deter Jamar from holding and talking to her. Serena was actually surprised by his interest in her daughter. She knew they were good friends, but she always thought her pregnancy was the reason they never grew closer.

When it was time to leave, Serena walked him outside and admired his Porsche. It was metallic silver with nary a dent or scratch.

"You drove the Porsche to school?"

He shook his head. "No. I had too much stuff to take. My mom and dad drove me in the SUV. But I'm going to drive it when I go back after Christmas." Even his voice was a little deeper than it had been before.

"You'll be the most popular freshman on campus, when you pull up in that ride," Serena guessed.

He grinned and shrugged. "I doubt that."

They stood on the porch watching each other for a moment. Serena sensed he had something to say, so she waited.

"I want to apologize," he told her.

She frowned. "For what?"

"For what happened to us after prom," he said.

Serena shook her head. "What are you talking about? You didn't do anything wrong."

"Yeah, I did. I had feelings for you, and I felt like you had feelings for me, too. But I backed away because of what people in my life wanted me to do."

Serena was surprised by the revelation, but not really. "Who? Your parents?"

He nodded. "My dad always told me I was old enough to make my own decisions, especially when it came to girls. But he gave me his opinion and said I should probably take his advice with this one. And I did."

Serena took a deep breath and let it out slowly. She didn't have to ask what advice his father had given him. After what happened at the prom, his whole family probably thought Serena was a harlot. She knew that she wasn't, but she couldn't fault them for thinking that way.

"It's okay," she said. "It was a long time ago. I'm not mad at you."

"It's not about being mad," he said. "It's about following our hearts and knowing what God's true plan for us is. On prom night, I knew it was you. But I turned my back anyway."

"You, what do you mean, you knew it was me?"

"I knew that I loved you," Jamar professed. "I knew that whatever you had done in the past was not enough to make me stop loving you. I felt like we were meant to be together. Did you ever feel that way, too?"

Goose bumps sprouted on every inch of Serena's body. Her blood began to flow fast and hot. Jamar continued to stare at her. She felt completely exposed, as if he could see into her very soul. Her heart ached for him. She was sure he could hear it beating and yearning.

She shook her head slowly.

He didn't believe her. He stepped closer and placed both of his hands on her sides. His touch was like fire. She flinched, but she didn't pull away. His beautiful face blurred as her eyes filled with tears.

"I don't wanna... I don't want to hurt," she said, speaking softly.

He said, "I would never hurt you."

She continued to shake her head. He didn't know how many times he hurt her in the past, how many times she stared at their prom pictures and wondered why – why did he kiss her if he didn't want to be with her? Why did he do so much to make their night special, if he wasn't falling in love with her, like she was falling for him?

"If you don't want to try, I understand," he said. "But I don't believe God brought us together just so we could go to the prom. I've never stopped loving you, Serena. I told my dad I was wrong to let you go. Tell me you want to be with me, too. I promise I'll never hurt you again."

Serena felt her blood flow even hotter as it mended all the pieces of her broken heart, making it whole again. She nodded and then looked up in time to close her eyes as Jamar's lips pressed against hers. She sighed. His kiss made the ground shake beneath them. She would've sworn she saw stars behind her closed eyelids.

Her whole body felt weak. But Jamar was strong. His hands moved to her back, and he held her up when she thought she would fall.

"I love you," he whispered between kisses. "I never stopped. I always will."

Serena was so overwhelmed, she barely had the strength to tell him "I love you, too."

ABOUT THE AUTHOR

Keith Thomas Walker, known as the Master of Romantic Suspense and Urban Fiction, is the author of nearly two dozen novels, including *Life After, Dripping Chocolate, The Realest Ever* and *Brick House*. Keith's books transcend all genres. He has published romance, urban fiction, mystery/thriller, teen/young adult, Christian, poetry and erotica. Originally from Fort Worth, he is a graduate of Texas Wesleyan University. Keith has won or been nominated for numerous awards in the categories of "Best Male Author," "Best Romance," and "Author of the Year," from several book clubs and organizations. Visit him at www.keithwalkerbooks.com.

CPSIA information can be obtained at www.ICGtesting.com
Printed in the USA
LVOW10s1629090715

445621LV00003B/546/P